TALES FROM THE DARK
HEART EMPORIUM

RICHARD LONG

COPYRIGHT© 2019 by

Richard Alan Long

All rights reserved

No part of this publication may be reproduced or transmitted in any form or by any electronic or mechanical means, including photocopying, recording or by any information storage or retrieval system, without the express written permission of the authors. Please do not encourage the piracy of copyrighted material in violation of the authors' rights.

This publication is a work of fiction. Names, characters, places, businesses and incidents are either the product of the authors' imaginations or are used fictitiously. Any resemblance or reference made to actual places, businesses, events or persons, living or dead, is entirely coincidental.

Copyright Richard Long 2019 except 'Indiscretions' 'The Haunted Ones' and 'Wicked Ways' Copyright Richard Long and Richard Raven.

'The Salesman' first appeared in the Hellbound Books release '*Demons, Devils and Denizens of Hell vol*

2' in 2017. 'Indiscretions' and 'The Haunted Ones' were first published in paperback by Richard Raven in his collection '*The Order*' in 2018.

ACKNOWLEDGEMENTS

Thank you, Margaret Bauer, for editing all stories in this collection except 'Indiscretions' and 'Wicked Ways' edited by Theresa Scott-Matthews

Artwork by Chris Ridley

Author Photo by Vicki Kennedy

Thanks to author and friend Richard Raven for working with me on three of the stories in this collection

Thank you Lori Cardille for all your support with my writing

Thanks to everyone who has purchased, read and supported my work

For Ann, Ruth and Grace

You are my world

I love you so much

For Keeps

For Always

CONTENTS

1. Welcome to the Emporium 1
2. About a Witch 12
3. World's Apart 43
4. Indiscretions 78
5. The Haunted Ones 116
6. The Long Distance Call 148
7. Survivors 164
8. The Salesman 173
9. The Priest and the Witch 188
10. Wicked Ways 197
11. Footsteps 249
12. The Emporium is Yours 270

WELCOME TO THE EMPORIUM

Dumbark was a cruel town, with unforgiving streets. No one cared; memories didn't exist because this had never been a happy place. Everyone lived, if you could call it that. The sky was always grey and cloudy; the rivers always brown and rancid. Some said the only good thing about Dumbark was a road that ran straight through the middle of it to the city of New Grace.

Everyone born in the town was working their best to leave and the ones that managed never came back, not even to visit family.

The kid had found his way into the town by desire. They'd told him at the work house that if you were quick, you could steal enough bread from the baker's cart before he'd notice. If he noticed you, worse if he caught you, he would choke you until your face turned bloated and purple.

The kid was hungry and the bread was worth the risk. He'd be whipped if the overseer discovered he'd left. Worse, he might be taken to the room with the orange door. He'd seen others taken there; some never came back and the ones who did never spoke again.

Hunger was driving the boy.

He made it into the town early, before anyone but the workers would be awake. Chimneys blew smoke and from the docks, he could hear shouts and vulgarities. He was bitter, clasping his arms around himself. The work house for all its faults was always warm and the floors smooth wood, not these cobbled streets that hurt his leather wrapped feet. He'd never witnessed cold like this. It was worse than feeling hungry. Still he walked on. Around the back of shop fronts, the smell of rotting fish hit him. Fish was the main source of food in Dumbark. Dragged from the brown river, the fishes looked nothing like normal creatures. These all had tough green skin, red deep-set eyes and razor teeth the colour of mustard. They could bite and take a finger or two, although they never fed on humans.

The kid made his way along the cobbled street. Dim light poured from windows in pools as he past. He glanced in one to find a man with fluffy red hair rolling multi-coloured slabs of candy. His mouth watered. He'd never tasted it. He'd been told it was like placing a piece of heaven in your mouth. One of his friends called Velm, had swallowed a fairy once, or so he claimed. He said that was the sweetest taste he'd ever experienced but candy was a very close second.

    Then the boy smelt it, faint but it was there, the smell of bread. Even over the grotesque fish smell he could smell it. A few shops along he saw the bread cart. It was loaded ready to be taken out for deliveries. Slowly he approached it, his stomach tearing itself apart in anticipation. He looked around and saw no one. The baker's door was closed. This was his chance. Shaking he grabbed a bread baton wrapped in wax paper. It was warm to the touch. It smelt exquisite. Quickly he put it under his arm and took another…and another…

As he turned to leave he saw briefly the dark shape and then felt the intense pain in his temple.

*

When he opened his eyes, the bread was all over the ground, dirty but still looking great. Some of it was splashed with blood. He looked up to find a man the size and width of a door. How could such a big hulk have snuck up so softly? The giant's eyes were burning with rage, his mouth was a mere slit, closed tight with anger. In his hand was a club, the end of it stained red and black. He was going to kill the boy, the kid knew that. Holding his hands up would be futile but he did it anyway.

'Put your filthy hands down lad and I'll make this quick.'

The boy dropped his hands in defeat,

hoping to find some compassion.

The giant smiled and lifted the thick, heavy club. Pretty soon the boy's life of twelve years would be over. He didn't have time to reflect. If he had, he would have remembered the only memory he savoured; a woman, his mother, cradling him by a warm fire. Babies can't remember that far back, but he did. Somehow, he did.

The club came down fast and the boy closed his eyes.

There was no impact.

The boy opened his eyes and stared in disbelief. The giant was still, the tip of a cut-glass sword held under his many chins. The holder was a man dressed in a black cloak. All the boy could see was the stranger's white as porcelain wrist and hand. The giant gazed at the cloaked figure. He was scared, troubled. It wasn't all down to the sword either. The man whispered something the boy couldn't hear to which the giant nodded.

'Get up boy you're coming with me,' said the stranger in a chilling soft voice.

Slowly the stranger moved the sword from the giant and turned to the boy. The boy looked up but couldn't see the face under the hood. He did see the giant lifting his club again, ready to smash the stranger's head. Before the boy could signal to the stranger, a hand flew up, holding the sword and then fell back down again in one fast and graceful motion. Suddenly the giant's throat erupted in crimson rivers, his life gushing out in front of him.

The boy didn't see the sword hit. Had the tip done all that violence in one quick swish?

'Come on boy, we have a long way to travel.'

The boy nodded. Suddenly his little life was full of possibilities.

'I am Arn,' said the boy trembling.

The stranger leant forward and the boy suddenly saw his face. The stranger was a Nigh. No one had seen them, they were a myth. The boy didn't believe in them. But he'd heard the stories. The Nigh were travellers; some said they had travelled from different worlds and times. The stranger had blackened eyes and white eggshell skin. Lips blue as delphinium flowers. They were known in the stories as the dark ones. Nothing they did was good and when they summoned you, nothing good would come of it. The boy shivered, with more than the cold. Still he got up, and took a few batons of bread with him. The giant stood motionless watching the two leave and then gazing down at the deep red river all around him.

'Call me Artaud,' said the stranger.

Artaud led the boy Arn through the town. Over the wet cobbled streets and through archways that spun here and there. The boy was fascinated by the many shops he passed but not so much by the beggars playing cards in a dirty doorway. They played for teeth, rotting and yellowed husks the boy doubted were human.

Eventually he came to a market. Sellers were shouting for customers. A woman was showing her breasts, both were sagging and covered in red sores. The boy's eyes glanced from stall to stall. Some sold books, others rare coins and weapons and another claimed to have unicorn bones crushed and bottled to cure any ailment. The stranger walked on and the boy followed.

They stopped outside a small black tepee. It rose up above their heads but didn't look big. The boy doubted more than three people could sit inside comfortably. The entrance covered with a cloth of rich red and gold tapestry. The stranger dragged it to the side and motioned for the boy to enter and when the boy looked in, there was nothing to see but darkness.

Begrudgingly Arn stepped inside.

*

Arn was in a shop or bazaar. Jugs and glasses hung from the ceiling, some shining emerald green inside, clearly magic. The floor was carpeted in patterns of swirling green that hurt his eyes when he stared for too long. There was a counter, filled with oddities in jars and bowls. Some moving.

The noise from outside had gone instantly. Sunlight poured through the two large windows and something terrifying moved outside to the sound of a heavy drone. Arn walked closer to the dirty window. His mouth hung open in horror. Continuously passing this way and that in front of the shop were large steel frames on wheels, people sitting in them behind glass. The chariots moved fast and slow and then fast. He hadn't seen anything like it. The world behind them was filled with grey buildings. This made no sense. The boy had seen the market and knew a field lay behind it filled with the king's finest horses.

'Those are cars boy, we are no longer in Dumbark,' said the voice behind him softly.

The boy turned to see the slender figure of the Nigh. It had removed its shroud and wore a black shirt and matching trousers that clung to the body like lacquered paint. Artaud's skin was white but with an almost blue shine to it. His neck long and slender. It was the basic shape of a man, but this creature wasn't human.

'Don't be scared of me Arn, I will not hurt you.'

'I've heard stories about your kind' said

Arn.

'We are travellers, the collectors of stories. We archive worlds and times, so that others may find these records, long after we have departed. This is my shop, where I store them.'

The boy looked around the shop. Against the length of each wall were tables draped in red silk. On these, side by side one another were glass cases with mahogany frames. Arn walked towards them. In the cases lay objects on red silk plinths. Some he recognised and others he did not. In one was a book called Sense and Sensibility. In another glass case was an object with a circular shape in its centre that hand numbers around it.

'That is a telephone,' said Artaud calmly.

'What does it do?' asked the boy stepping closer.

The stranger walked forward and placed a delicate hand on the glass. 'This like everything else in my emporium comes from a story I have collected. All the stories come from out there, in this world. Some from different times, some from alternative times and I have listened to them all.'

'I don't understand. I don't know this world,' said the boy, his voice sounding fragile.

'I am going to teach you about it. I am old now, too old. I can't gather these stories anymore.

So, you will.'

'But I can't do that, I am not like you. I don't live half as long as your kind.'

With that the stranger laughed a long haunting sound and then stared back in fascination at the boy. His black eyes seemed to flicker and react.

'In time, you will be just like me. A dark-hearted old fool with an admiration for a good story and a pleasure for the macabre. This gift I give you is a blessing not a curse.'

The boy's eyes shifted to a strange painting above the stranger. On it a naked woman was standing on a hillside.

'That is an interesting story. I think you will like it.'

The boy smiled. Besides the counter at the top end of the square shaped room, and the tables down each side, there was nothing in the centre. A big empty space. The boy looked up, the ceiling was so dark he couldn't quite see it, and when he thought he did he wondered if it was mirrored, or that the dark face looking down at him was a demon. He looked away, pushed it from his mind.

Whatever lay ahead sure beat the workhouse thought the boy. But regardless of stories, his stomach craved something else far more.

'Of course, you're hungry,' said the stranger as if he had read his mind. 'Please allow me.'

Suddenly a green mist arose from the centre of the room and when it faded there was a table. Plates stacked high with roasted chickens, fresh apples, grapes, peppered meats and batons of warm bread. There were goblets too with red liquids and tankards of foaming beer. The boy had never tasted beer. He was too young for such delights.

'Is that for me?' asked the boy, hoping.

'Yes, you can eat it as I tell you about this world and some of my favourite tales. Only go easy on the red rope liquorice. It can stick in the throat.'

'But I might not understand what you say,' said the boy edging towards the food. 'I have no idea what they are,' he said and pointed out of the window.

'They are cars. I'll tell you all about them and everything else here and when I am done you will record more stories for the emporium.'

Arn picked up a chicken leg and turned to Artaud. His mind racing with questions.

'Will we be here long?'

With that Artaud smiled and sat down.
'Long enough that you might want to sit down.'

ABOUT A WITCH

The two brothers had been parked beside the primary school for the last forty minutes. Neither of them spoke but that was all right. They didn't mind sitting in silence; besides they could just about read each other's mind anyway.

Carl, the eldest, was looking straight ahead at the row of houses on George Street. He was thinking about which house they should stay in and then, as always, his mind switched to thoughts of Jackie.

James was looking at the school. It wasn't the one he had attended but it looked similar. There was a body of a dog lying on its grey steps, a morbid welcome if you ever did see one. Part of him wanted to exit the car and move the dog but in his mind, he knew it was pointless. They'd seen dozens of dead animals on their journey, besides where the hell would he move it to.

'Come on,' said Carl, and both men got out of the car, taking what little pleasure they could from stretching their legs.

James could smell the late October air and it made him feel remorseful. He began to think about Jackie. In his mind, she was always dancing. He pushed the thought aside and took out his cigarettes. Passing a white stick to his brother, he lit his own and inhaled deeply feeling a moment of relaxation as the smoke filled his lungs.

Carl lit his cigarette and walked around the Citroen, checking the front tyres. James walked towards the school a few short steps. He wondered what the dog's name had been.

Both brothers were in their twenties and both were English although, with Carl's darker features and heavy-set frame, he always got asked if he was Italian.

James was a similar height to his brother, but his body wasn't toned or looked after like Carl's. James had always found comfort in food and that comforting had begun to show over the years, in his rounded frame and large thighs. There were no dark features either; James was white to the point of pasty, even in his blonde hair, which had started to recede. He hated it when women said they couldn't believe Carl was his brother.

'We can stay in that house with the blue door on it,' Carl shouted across to James.

James turned around and walked back to the car. He had hoped that they might have reached their destination by nightfall. Perhaps not.

'You drive down there, I want to stretch my legs some more,' said Carl, walking across the road towards the rows of houses.

James got into the car and pressed play on the CD player. Something by Aerosmith filled the car; it had been Jackie's favourite. He hated rock music but that didn't matter. All that mattered was Jackie.

He started the car and drove down the road, passing his brother, until after a few seconds, he was outside the house with the blue door. In the garden, he noticed a stuffed lion, similar to the one from the Disney film. Next to it and splashed with mud, was a child's play pen. Most of the wooden bars were broken away. James quickly pushed the idea of how they could have been broken out of his mind.

Carl was nearly there now and almost finished his cigarette. He flicked it across the road and wiped the thin line of sweat from his top lip.

The two of them took the three bags from the boot of the car with James carrying the two lightest. James, surprised that the blue door wasn't locked, placed each bag in the tiny hallway. When he returned to the car, Carl was standing motionless looking into the back seat.

James swallowed and his throat made a clicking sound.

In the back seat, propped up with several pillows and wearing a new dress she had purchased from 'Next' before she died, was Jackie.

Both men stared at their seventeen-year-old sister, lost in their own remembrance.

She was still pretty. Even though her skin was now turning an alarming grey colour, you could still see her beauty. Her long black hair, which had now lost its shine, still had great volume to compliment her face. Her eyes were closed but behind the lids they were large and hazel; eyes that had melted and broken a few hearts in her short seventeen years on the planet. Although the brothers had never let her have boyfriends to visit, they weren't naive enough to think she went to cinema with her girlfriends every weekend.

James opened the car door and looked at his brother. His breathing was fast and the panic was already setting into his eyes. Carl reached forward and placed a hand on his shoulder.

'You go inside and put the kettle on, see if there's anything in there to eat. I'll take care of Jackie.'

In the house, which James couldn't help but notice was very organised, unlike the other places where they had stayed, he filled the kettle and checked the cupboards. There were a few tins of beans and soups, which he took out and placed on the worktop. In the fridge, which hadn't had power for weeks there was a coffee-cake still boxed. Opening it, the cake was stale but probably edible. Even if Carl didn't want any, James felt like a slice wouldn't hurt him.

Altogether, along with the cake and tinned goods, he found a handful of Penguin biscuits, several oatmeal bars, tins of beans and best of all, two tins of corned beef and tinned ham.

As he poured the tea into two cups, he heard his brother panting as he carried Jackie over the threshold. Part of him wanted to go and help but he knew he'd only get in the way. He was always told he got in the way.

Carl was already in the living room now, swearing and then apologising to his sister for his profanity.

'Why did you put her tennis shoes on her?' shouted Carl. 'She hated them!'

James ignored his bother and continued making the tea.

'Did you even check the house to make sure it's empty!' yelled Carl again.

James didn't answer. Of course the house was empty. Everywhere was empty.

*

They ate corn beef and beans that night and then smoked heavily. Jackie had been laid out in the lounge on a table James didn't' think was strong enough but had let Carl place her there anyway. If it broke and she fell it wouldn't really be the end of the world. After all, James thought, hadn't the end of the world already happened?

'When we find her, I want to tell her all about Jackie,' said Carl.

'If we do find her,' said James sharply. 'We don't even know if Eve O'Grady exists and if she does, we don't know if she can help us like she did all those other people.'

'It's no use having doubts now. Jesus, don't you want to see Jackie again?' demanded Carl. 'Don't you miss her and want her back?'

'Of course, I want her back!' shouted James 'I want her back more than anything. I'm just saying that by doing it this way, there might be a risk.'

'You were there when we met that old man and his kid,' James continued.

'That kid didn't look right though, Carl. You must agree.'

'You're having doubts now!' yelled Carl, making James sit upright. 'You're having doubts like you fucking always do! Even before the end, you had doubts about everything. That kid had come back from the fucking dead. Of course he wasn't right. It takes time.'

Carl walked across to his brother and knelt by his side.

'You will see I am right and that Eve O'Grady can and will help us.'

'Fine then,' whispered James, lying back down on the sofa. 'We should have found her by morning.'

Carl walked to the window and looked out.

'You know, this place looks like home.'

James didn't answer.

'I miss our old house. Last week I found a kid hunting for food in an empty shop. I begged him to let me help him but he wouldn't leave the store. Told me his brother was dead in the back room. I couldn't bring myself to check but I think the kid had been eating his brother to stay alive.'

'That's awful. Worse than what we saw on the bridge.'

'Isn't nothing worse than what we saw on the bridge,' whispered Carl looking down at his hands, turning them over and flicking at his fingernails.

'This really is the end isn't it?' asked James, his voice wavering.

Carl didn't answer; he was looking in the mirror at himself. James thought about saying something about Jackie but knew there was no point.

'I'm going to check on Jackie.' said Carl leaving the room.

James turned over, wishing hard he could go to sleep although knowing no sleep would find him. When he closed his eyes he pictured Jackie, glowing brightly like the best thing he'd ever seen, wearing her alabaster dress as new as the day she'd bought it. Then he saw the unfocussed look in her eyes. They were still hazel and dazzling, but there was something missing and even worse, there was something that had been replaced.

James opened his own eyes and couldn't help but think. If he ever saw Jackie again, what would he say to her? What would be the first thing he said to her?

*

In the morning Carl had already washed, eaten some oatmeal bars and escorted Jackie back into the car, by the time James had woken from his pitiful two and half hours sleep.

There was blue sky outside, which was odd for October, but at the same time it felt good. James stood on the front porch enjoying an Embassy filter. Autumn leaves were blowing up and down the street in swirls of gold and brown. There was something about swirling leaves and that autumn morning air that you couldn't get enough of, thought James. It made everything seem normal again, even if it did only last a minute.

Carl started the engine whilst James closed the door, kicking himself for wondering if he should lock it. Up the street he could see the school and as he walked towards the car, he wondered if the dog was still on its steps. The idea of taking the dog with them popped into his mind but he knew that was probably one of the worst ideas he could think of.

The drive to Furlonger was done mostly in silence. Occasionally, Carl would ask for a cigarette or for a drink but not often. James didn't feel like talking much either. Before the end, they barely talked anyway. It was the end that had pulled people apart and the end that had brought them together. James did love his brother though, deeply and sometimes scarily. He knew if Carl died he'd be alone in the world; in a world he wasn't sure he could handle alone. He knew he might meet someone else but it was unlikely. Most of the people that had survived were cautious of making new friends and either stayed in their small groups like he and Carl did or they travelled alone. Then, of course, there was the other small percentage who liked to castrate people and hang them from bridges.

'We're nearly there if these directions are right' said Carl.

James looked around. The town of Furlonger was no different from any other town they'd passed through. Shops stood either boarded up or looted and James couldn't help but smile when he saw the still glowing arches of the McDonalds sign. It seemed to him that true evil never dies.

'I think at the next turning there should be a pub called the Ale Taster and then a few miles after that, we should see Eve's house.'

God, they were really doing this. James felt a cold sweat building up on the back of his neck. Carl, on the other hand, was composed, almost too focused thought James.

They turned a corner and the town ended abruptly, cutting off into countryside, but as it did, there stood a large, blue, thatched-roofed house; not a huge, great house, just a small one, painted blue.

A wall, about six feet high and topped with barbed-wire, surrounded the house. There was a single iron gate, gothic in its style, which didn't fit with the style of the house.

When they pulled up inches from the gateway, they saw a queue of no more than five or six people. The most people the two brothers had seen in weeks.

Carl swung the car round, parking as close as he could. He wasted no time, getting out as soon as he had applied the hand brake.

The gates were wide enough for people to step through but not enough for a car.

Carl had Jackie in his arms, carrying her now as if she weighed no more than that of a small child. They walked slowly round the car and joined the end of the queue.

In front of them there was a tall, muscular young man with long blonde hair, which fell in great waves down his shoulders. In his arms, he held what looked like a baby, although all James could see was one small pale hand, the rest was concealed in cloth.

'Not long now sweetheart,' said the man to the baby, before gently kissing it on the forehead. James swallowed.

He knew the last thing on earth he wanted to see was a dead baby. He looked further up the line. In front of the muscular guy was a man dressed in what looked like his wedding suit. He held a woman dressed in a once white but now grey, wedding dress. Clearly, from the way she leaned against him, she was dead. He held her like a mannequin. The way she was stiffened with rigor mortis looked almost comical to James, until his eyes focussed on her legs, which were blue and ink-blotched with congealed blood.

'Not much longer now, sweetheart' said the muscular guy to his concealed child.

Carl shook his head and looked at James; they were both thinking the same thing.

'Daddy loves you.'

James looked at his feet but couldn't cover his ears from the sound the muscular guy's lips made every time he kissed the child's forehead.

At the front of the queue half out of sight, was a woman sobbing gently. By her side was a short, stocky man wearing a Manchester United shirt. In his hand, he held a doll by its arm, which spun loosely in a circular motion.

James caught the doll's face as it turned outward and then spun so the back of its head pointed towards him. The face would haunt him forever now, he was sure of that.

'He will break the arm swinging her like that,' said Carl, to which James mimed the words 'forget it' and turned himself away from the direction of the front entrance.

'Don't worry, darling. Daddy won't let you go,' said the muscular man, before the kissing sound was made again.

Before either of them could react, the door to the house was opened and a family came out. Three kids who looked no older than eight ran past the line and down towards the open gates. They played tag as they went, not letting the stink of death get in the way of them having fun. Kids adapt, thought James.

Following behind the kids were the parents.

Everyone in the queue fell silent. James wanted to look up to see who had been awakened by Eve O'Grady but found he couldn't do it. He just couldn't look. Somehow, he knew it was the woman, and no matter how much he wanted to, he couldn't look into her eyes as she walked down the line. There was something he didn't want to see. Then, he caught a glimpse of the child swinging from the man's hand like a doll, its dead eyes watching him as the kissing sound in front of him smacked, 'Daddy love you'

When the woman did pass James with her husband helping her, there was a sudden odour, something that reminded James of the dirt he'd dig up in the woods as a child, burying his toys. James wondered if that was the smell of being awakened. If that was the smell of the living dead, maybe it wasn't so bad.

When the family had gone and the sound of their car engine driving away could be heard, James felt a slight sense of relief but this wasn't long lived.

Suddenly a man dressed all in white came from the entrance, holding a clipboard. He stood looking at the queue and then asked for silence, which was pointless, since everyone was silent already.

He looks like Johnny Depp, James thought. He's a dead ringer.

'Anyone bringing their dead here with severe wounds to the body must leave now. Eve can't help you,' said Johnny, who sounded nothing like the actor. 'Anyone coming here with their dead having wounds to internal organs must leave now, Eve can't help you.'

There was suddenly some ruckus from the two people at the front of the queue. The man in Manchester top was shouting at his partner. James looked at Carl who was staring back at him.

'Don't worry we're okay' Carl said and then kissed Jackie on her forehead, something that morbidly sounded the same as the man kissing his dead baby. James looked at his sister. She lay into Carl like a drunk. Her mouth was slightly open, the way it used to be when she slept. There had been times when James watched her lying in the arms of death and prayed that she would open her eyes. Sometimes, he thought he could almost will it. Looking at her now, he wished it was true.

The couple was arguing now and the man with clipboard was alongside them. James tried but couldn't hear what they were saying but whatever it was made the man in the Manchester top angry until, finally, he took the rag doll child he was swinging and threw it across the yard where it landed in a sickening thud.

'Hey man! There's no need for that!'
shouted the muscular guy in front of James and Carl.

The guy in the football shirt was now crying, great heavy sobs that cut to the bone to hear; he walked away from the line and left his wife standing. Slowly, she walked over to where her child had been thrown and picked him up. James expected a great wail of tears like they had heard from her partner but there was nothing. The woman cradled the child and walked away with him.

'Leave it!' shouted the husband, who by now was standing outside the gates.

His wife paused and then dropped the child before walking through the gates to her husband.

'You can't just leave her here,' shouted the Johnny Depp lookalike with the clipboard, but it fell on deaf ears.

'Right, now for the rest of you,' Johnny shouted in a pissed off tone, 'the third rule. Anyone whose dead has been dead for longer than a week must leave now, Eve can't help you.'

Carl darted his head at James.

They both knew it had been longer than a week since she'd died.

'Don't say anything,' hissed Carl, as Johnny walked towards them. When he stood beside them, he didn't speak. He looked at Jackie, wrote something on his clipboard and went back into the house, signalling the guy in the wedding suit and his partner to follow him.

James looked across at the dead kid lying in a heap. He couldn't see his face and that was better, but like the dog that he'd seen lying on the school steps, he felt that this wasn't right. Someone should move him.

They waited an hour, maybe two, and then the wedding suit guy came out with his wife, who was now very much alive. Carl stopped him as he passed and asked what happened. The muscular guy was looking back, also concerned.

'She is alive isn't she? My beautiful wife is back!' cried the man.

But the woman looked out of it. Like she'd drunk too much alcohol and could barely walk. She opened her eyes and looked at James. The whites of her eyes were completely bloodshot. She looked exorcist scary.

Johnny Depp quickly ran from the building towards the wedding party.

'She had been dead too long!' he screamed, at which the bride and groom quickly rushed away awkwardly, the groom keeping his wife steady.

'She is your problem now!' ordered Depp.

James watched the couple and as they turned to walk out of the gates, the bride glanced back him. She was smiling. It looked awful. Demented and damned.

'Next!' ordered Johnny Depp.

The muscular guy walked slightly bow-legged into the house leaving the two brothers and their dead kid sister outside.

'D'you think I've got time for a smoke?' asked James.

'You kidding. You've probably got time for a whole pack the length of time this will take.'

James nodded and took the carton from his pocket before realising he didn't actually want one. Still he took one out and shakily popped it into his mouth anyway.

'What do we tell her if she asks how long Jackie has been dead for?' asked James.

'The truth' said Carl, 'we tell her that Jacks died less than a week ago. Besides, what the hell does a few days make? Nothing at all.'

'How do we know that Carl?' asked James.

'Stop asking questions.'

'We don't know what will happen if we take her in there and the witch…'

'Don't call her a fucking witch.'

'Then tell me what she is, for god sake! That's exactly what she is. This act she'll perform isn't medical. Jesus, did you see that woman's eyes?'

'Shut up!' shouted Carl angrily.

'I think we should leave.' said James abruptly.

'I'm not letting Jackie go now,' said Carl bitterly.

'Don't you think I want Jackie back? But look at the world we'll be bringing her back to; it's as dead as that kid over there.'

'Enough!' shouted Carl so loud it could have woken the dead.

'Yeah, whatever you say brother, you're just feeling guilty. She's dead because of you,' said James, regretting it the second the words left his mouth and almost instantly feeling a hard slap across his face, connecting fully with the right cheek.

James was stunned. His brother had never hit him, not even when they were kids. His face felt hot and enlarged. A rage burned through his veins.

'I shouldn't have done that,' said Carl.

James didn't reply. He feared that if he opened his mouth, he would say something he'd regret. Instead, he walked away a few paces, lit another cigarette and inhaled it deeply.

After an hour, it was the muscular guy's turn to leave the house. He was smiling. His child, who was still wrapped in his arms, was crying.

James smiled and looked at his brother who smiled back. Everything felt wonderful and alive with hope. The muscular guy walked past them and smiled a warm, kind smile. He had his baby back. James thought the kid's crying sounded like he was trying to say something, probably hungry. Still, it was a good healthy sound and as he walked past James, the muscular guy nodded down at his child. James looked and the baby looked healthy, its cheeks tinted red and eyes a warm blue colour.

At the doorway stood Johnny Depp – they were up next.

*

Johnny Depp had taken Jackie off for what he said was 'preparing'; something Carl didn't feel comfortable about.

They were told to wait in the main room and it wasn't at all what the brothers had expected. Firstly, it wasn't some sort of dark, candle-lit room, where Ouija boards and voodoo dolls lay scattered. Instead, they were in a normal-looking living room, which had all the modern-day appliances that any living room would have. There was a sofa, table and chairs, armchairs, a cabinet for drinks and, to James amazement, a television – which he presumed was just ornamental now.

Above the fireplace, an oil painting was hung, depicting an average looking landscape, although when James got closer, he noticed the painting wasn't at all behaving itself. Right in the centre, way back, almost out of sight, were a naked woman and man. The woman was holding onto the male's penis, as if leading him forward by it. That small image made the rest of the painting look cheap and juvenile.

*

When Eve O'Grady entered the room, James first noticed how much she looked like the woman in the oil painting.

Eve was a small woman in her late fifties with thick tattered locks of white hair. Yet, for her age, there were still the faint whispers of youthfulness in her features.

'Please have seat gentlemen. I know you have come a long way,' said the woman in a warm, soft voice that made both brothers feel more relaxed.

'So, please tell me about your loss,' she asked in that way a counsellor might ask a grieving relative. Carl went into detail about Jackie and had to keep stopping as he sank into telling the woman his sister's life story, which Eve seemed to enjoy nevertheless.

'She was out in the street,' interrupted James. 'There were these lights in the sky and she wanted to follow them.'

'Ah yes those lights declaring the end,' interrupted Eve. 'We never knew when or where they would strike next. I lost many friends to them.'

James cleared his throat. He had been there; he would tell them the story. He looked at his brother, who nodded.

'Well, she was walking and dancing as she does when she gets excited, and then there was a loud bang. It tore up the sky. I woke up in a bus shelter. I was bleeding all over but it was nothing major. Jackie wasn't so lucky,' James said, gasping to catch his breath. 'She wasn't blown up but I think she must have banged her head pretty badly on the way down because…'

'It was my fault,' interrupted Carl. 'I sent them both out to get me some cigarettes.'

'Nonsense,' said Eve. 'The end is unpredictable; everyone outside lost their life. There was no one to blame but the gases and carbons in the sky. No one else, you hear me! I thought the first time we saw those lights it would be the last. But, dear me, my friend Ruby fell fatal to them just last night.'

'I'm sorry…' said James but the old woman waved a hand to shut him up.

'So your sister never woke up, I know,' said Eve sounding motherly.

Both brother shook their heads.

From the kitchen came a strong fragrance of cooking meat. James stomach did a flip with hunger pains; it had been along time since he had smelt anything so good.

'It is rabbit you can smell,' said Eve in a matter of fact tone.

'It smells good,' said James, not sure when the last time was he'd had freshly cooked meat. Actually, he wasn't sure if he liked rabbit. He sure liked the smell though.

'Now, did my good man tell you the rules?' asked Eve.

Carl nodded and glanced at James, who was staring at the oil painting.

'Let's pretend your girl got shot in the belly and it made a right mess of her insides. It would be too much for me to put her right, said Eve. 'I have been known to fix broken legs and even the occasional fractured skull but sometimes, when a body is badly damaged, there is nothing I can do.'

'We understand' said Carl.

'What is worse, is if the person comes back to life and they are in so much pain that they wish they were dead, said Eve. 'Now if your girl had her stomach torn out and you didn't tell me...'

'We know,' said Carl, 'we know she'd be in a lot of pain.'

'I only tell you because if your girl hit her head she might wake up and suffer headaches for the rest of her life, or she might wake up and be comatose. There is no telling when it comes to head trauma. It might be easier if there were still doctors but it has been a long time since I saw one of those.'

'Well we don't know how badly she was

hit when she fell,' said James 'although it must have been bad because…well it killed her.'

Carl laughed a short sharp laugh, which James didn't like at all. It made his brother sound like he was losing his mind.

'Well if she returns and she is lost to you,' said Eve lifting her hands outward in a wave, 'then there is a simple action I can do to put her back under.'

'I don't know if she would like to be in the world if she constantly had headaches,' said James.

'If she has headaches she will be fine; they will fade over time,' said the woman, bringing a smile to Carl's face.

'When can we begin?' asked Carl.

'*I* begin soon; you two will wait here and eat,' laughed the woman humourlessly, before standing up and walking towards the door.

'How long does it take?' asked Carl.

'Patience boy, I have seen the awakening take as long as six hours or in less time it takes to tie your shoelaces,' said Eve.

'Yes, we understand,' said James 'and we have money.'

'Thank you, but I don't need anything, especially money. Please enjoy your meal when it comes and help yourself from the drinks cabinet,' said Eve. 'Oh and one last thing…'

'What is it?' said Carl panicking.

'You lads didn't lie to me did you?' asked Eve. 'Your girl hasn't been dead longer than a week, has she?'

'No,' said Carl not looking up, 'but what would happen if she had been dead longer? I'm only curious, that's all.'

'Then her mind may have been affected,' declared Eve. 'Such a long period of time does certain things to the mind and not just the mind. Remember I am awakening not just her human body but also her soul and we don't know where that has been, do we?'

Both brothers felt a shiver at the thought of the soul going places unknown and didn't notice when Eve left the room. They sat in silence; privately hoping things would go well. James thought about the woman in her bridal gown - her deep red eyes and that awful smile.

About twenty minutes later, their meals were delivered to the room by a young Asian male they hadn't seen before. Their plates were filled with tinned potatoes, carrots and peas, alongside two slices of rabbit meat covered in gravy.

Neither brother touched the food. They sat in deep in thought until James stood up and went to the window. Outside there was a long line of people, one of whom held a wheelbarrow, with stick-thin arms poking out from it.

James turned away and took his cigarettes out. He passed one to Carl, who popped it into his mouth, lit it and inhaled deeply.

They stayed silent for a long time until…

'What am I going to say to her James?' asked Carl.

James shook his head. 'Perhaps we will know when the time comes.'

'It scares me,' said Carl softly. 'The idea that her soul could have been to other places.'

'I know.'

They sat for a further two hours, not eating, or talking.

They only smoked.

*

After two hours, there was a shout from the hallway and then the door swung open and crashed against the wall. James could already see it was Eve before looking up. Her white mop of tattered her was reflected in the television screen.

'Both of you get out of my house now!' demanded Eve.

James and Carl stood up. Carl put his hand into his jeans pocket and brought out a wad of notes.

'If you think I want your money now, you're wrong!' she yelled loudly, taking away any youthfulness her face once had.

They walked for the door, James sure Eve would hit them as they passed her, but she didn't have to; her staring grey eyes seemed to hurt much more.

They walked into the hall expecting Eve to follow them but she didn't. She slammed the living room door behind them. The man holding the clipboard greeted them.

'Gentlemen,' he said indifferently.

James was about to speak and then noticed a dark droplet of blood on the man's forehead and couldn't help but wonder whether it was a puncture or someone else's blood.

'What happened, didn't it work?' asked Carl.

'You lied to us gentlemen. You disregarded the rules,' said the man, who now somehow looked less like Johnny Depp.

'But we didn't know,' said James.

'Yes, that's what they all say' said the man. 'Please, we now have to cancel all other appointments, so Mrs O'Grady can rest. So, if you would like to leave... or perhaps you can go out there and tell all those people why Eve O'Grady can't see them.'

'No we're leaving,' said Carl, 'but we're not going anywhere without my sister's body.'

The man's head suddenly flew back in a fit of laughter that sounded so childlike it was almost scary. 'She's ready and waiting you fools. One of our people has already put her in your car.'

Carl looked at James unsure.

'Is she dead?' asked James.

'Oh she's far worse than that,' laughed the man, as he walked past them to the door and down the two steps leading outside.

James rubbed his face. He could feel his whole body was shaking. He hoped that when they got to the car, Jackie would be dead.

The two brothers walked outside, ignoring the shouts and cries from the queue as Johnny Depp spoke to them.

'Maybe tomorrow,' James heard him say and then the place erupted in an array of cat calls, swearing and then dull thuds, which James felt scared to turn around to, as if it was the sound of someone getting a beating.

*

As they approached the car, Carl stopped and stared forward. James soon did the same. In the back of the car she was sitting, without the aid of a pillow to prop her up. Jackie was sitting there, looking out of the window at her two brothers. Carl saw his sister wasn't wearing her dress anymore, she was naked.

'They took her dress?' said Carl bitterly. 'Those animals stripped her naked.'

James then smiled at her and awaited a response but she didn't smile back, she just stared at them.

'Can you smell that?' asked James.
Carl didn't reply. He stood motionless.

*

James looked into the back of the car, where

Jackie was staring back at him, her once rosy cheeks now just as grey as they had been when they had brought her to this place.

'How are you feeling, sis?' he said and then regretted it. How would you feel if you had just woken up from death after three weeks?

'Are we going…' she said in a croaked, tired and old sounding voice '…play football in the street…,' she broke off in a fit of angry, painful coughs, which made James turn white and feel a fear he not felt since…

'I think we should drive away from this place,' James said and clicked in his seat belt.

Carl started the car.

'Is Casper home yet? I want to see Casper,' Jackie said.

James held his head against his hand and bit his lip. Casper had been her cat when she was six. She would always ask if he was home when she'd come home from school. Casper had died years ago.

'Has Robert phoned for me when I was at school?' she asked.

'No not yet he hasn't but there's still time,' said James.

Carl kept driving, not answering but not able to stop himself looking into the rear-view mirror. James didn't like the way his brother was shaking; it looked like he was cracking up, coming apart. The brother, who was always in control and never cried, was starting to fall apart. James felt scared.

'We were at the beach but it was raining and all I wanted to do was ditch them, so I could go to the party.'

They turned the corner and drove back onto Furlonger main street.

'I should have put breathing holes in the top. He shouldn't have died. I feel so guilty.'

Carl grimaced shaking his head.

'Keep it together,' said James.

'How the fuck can I when…?'

'I'm not supposed to drink; I had cider once at one of my brother's parties. You'd like my brother Carl, he's funny.'

James turned in his seat. The girl in the back looked and sounded like his sister but deep down he felt this wasn't his sister.

'I'm sorry but I don't think we can be friends anymore,' said Jackie coldly and then breathed a deep breath and started talking continuously…

'He said he was the hardest in school, perhaps the whole world.'

Beat

'One day I will have a birthday party that's better than Lucy Whitman's.'

Beat

'You won't believe what I found under my brother Carl's bed.'

Beat.

'Shut her up for god's sake!' yelled Carl.

'This was a gift from my mother, I never liked it.'

Beat.

Suddenly, her voice changed to one they didn't recognise and she spoke slowly in a lingering tone.

'These dark roads, where do they go Carl? Do all the spirits walk this way?'

'What the fuck does that mean? Oh shit, James. What have we done!' shouted Carl.

James noticed his brother was crying hysterically as the car swerved.

'Don't listen to her Carl,' ordered James. 'Christ that doesn't even sound like our Jackie.'

'All dark places lead to somewhere, don't they Carl?' she asked, her voice now deeper and hoarse.

'Oh fuck! I can't hear this…' said Carl driving faster.

'…and as all the king's roaches watched from below, so below, in the tunnels of hell.'

Carl screamed in anger, tears streaming down his face.

'Stop talking Jackie, just stop it. You have to snap out of this.'

A laugh suddenly escaped her; not hers, never hers. This sounded like the laugh of something he'd never heard before.

Carl screamed and just as James tried to control the steering wheel in his brother's hands, the car was drifting to the side of the road and towards an up turned Range Rover.

'I see you James. I see all of you!' said Jackie.

The car was getting faster now and James was screaming, as he elbowed his brother as hard as he could and tried to take control of the wheel.

James managed to swerve the car around the Range Rover and then again, this time around a badly parked white van.

'Carl I can't…' suddenly James stopped and saw the zigzag of five cars up ahead which he doubted he could control his way through from the passenger seat. He looked at his brother, who'd let go of the wheel, his face staring ahead despairingly. Trying, nevertheless, James kept control past the first set of cars but not the last small cherry red Volvo.

They hit and hit hard, spinning the Citroen like a toy.

After the smoke had settled James opened his eyes. James looked across and saw Carl, although it didn't look like his brother anymore. His jaw was broken and swinging comically. There was blood everywhere, pouring from his ears and the crushed mess where his nose had been.

'What time is the show tonight…'

James turned his head from Carl and saw Jackie in the rear-view. Christ, thought James. Whoever had sat Jackie in the car had taken the time to make sure her seatbelt was on, yet Carl his brother, couldn't do the same. He thought about undoing his own, but the icy pain in his leg would no doubt hurt a lot more. He'd have to build up to it.

Fuck, he thought. He knew the leg was broken. The only chance for help was Jackie who…

Suddenly there was nothing and for a long time it stayed that way until…

'Carl said it was his fault. He made us go out.'

James opened his eyes.

Trying to move was useless. His leg hurt too much. He turned and saw…Jackie was out of the car now standing in front of him.

She was completely naked except for her awful white tennis shoes.

James watched a she walked up the main street, drifting into the middle of the road, draped in October sunlight. She shone and for a second, making James think she was an angel. Despite everything, it was good to see her alive again. No, it was better than good, it was amazing. He turned to his brother Carl, the brother who had always looked after him.

'She looks great doesn't she?' he asked, feeling that Carl would have been made up if he could have seen Jackie now.

Slowly he reached for his cigarettes and put one in his mouth. He took his Zippo from his shirt pocket and lit it, inhaling deeply.

In the distance, he could still see his sister walking naked up the main street swaying from side to side. Autumn leaves were blowing up and down the street in swirls of gold and brown and Jackie was right there in the middle of them. There was something about swirling leaves and that autumn morning air that you couldn't get enough of, thought James. It made everything seem normal again, even if it did only last a minute.

WORLDS APART

Roger Barber thought Kirby Graveyard and Crematorium was the most beautiful place on earth, especially in the summer. Not that the thirteen year old had ever been abroad and experienced the Niagara Falls or the stunning beauty of the Eiffel Tower but in his world, which consisted of the town of the Kirby, this place was paradise.

Better yet, it was his.

Always empty and without noise or other kids the Crem (as everyone called it) was a place unlike home or school. There weren't any bullies here and if there were, they were all dead.

Roger thought the crematorium itself looked like a small church and on days when someone was being cremated he'd often hear church hymns playing, although on some days, he'd also hear Celine Dion and Robbie Williams.

The entrance had a huge oak oval door but he'd never been inside. Roger liked to walk around the back of the building. There, he found a stone wall about knee high and nearby a small grassy knoll. It didn't bother him that this was a place for the dead. His mother always told him the dead couldn't hurt the living, only the living could do that, like his father had hurt her.

The knoll, a small patch of grass unoccupied by graves, caught the summer sun beautifully. Roger had seen people dressed in black standing on it before a service.

Death was hard on people. Roger had lost his father and his uncle Gary, although his father wasn't dead. He just had a new family in Washington. He used to send letters and money but that had stopped a few years ago, and Roger was starting to forget what he looked like. His uncle Gary though, he'd never forget him, although just thinking about him dying, wiped out by a heart attack in his sleep, made Roger feel sad.

He had seen his uncle Gary after he died and regretted it ever since. The body he saw looked nothing like his uncle. The face was different. The lips looked paper thin and his hair colourless. His uncle always had rosy cheeks and fine red hair that captured sunlight, making it look golden. His mother wouldn't let him go to the funeral and he was secretly glad. He didn't want to see his uncle that awful way again.

Instead, he tried to remember him the best way he could. When they'd play football in the back garden, his mother stood on the step smoking. That was a good memory. Sometimes he wished those long summer nights would never end, but like everything, they did. It all ended one day when Roger came home to find Gary sitting in the armchair, motionless. A can of Sprite in his hand. His eyes staring forward at nothing.

Being here at the crem wasn't strange or morbid. Roger actually didn't think of the dead when he was here. This was his escape from the world – but not in the way the dead had escaped. Roger just loved to sit on the grassy knoll, reading his kindle and scoffing chocolate.

His mother said there was nothing wrong with kids having a sweet tooth even when she was diabetic and had to stab herself with an insulin pen, chocolate couldn't hurt you according to Pamela Barber. It was better than kids smoking or taking drugs.

But the chocolate had made Roger fat.

Not chubby or baby fat. He was the other fat. The kind that the kids scoffed at and the kind his P.E. teacher Mr. Duncan called disgusting when Roger ran cross-country and almost collapsed. It was a product of eating too much. Damn those Reese's were the worst. It made him sad and when he was sad he'd buy a carrier bag full of ket (a local term for sweets) and play truant from Kirby Secondary School. It was mostly chocolate bars, crisps and a can of cola he'd purchase from Dashers corner shop, and it always came in dark blue carrier bags.

By lunch, he'd have sat and made his way through all of it. That was why his class mate, Ben McDaniels, called him a fat cunt in front of Donna

Grey. That was why they laughed when he ran in PE and that was why no girls ever looked twice at him.

Not ever.

Not even when he bought some hair gel that looked like ectoplasm and combed his hair into a wet look over his eyes like Justin Bieber. Girls still saw his fat face blooming under a cool haircut. This hurt like hell.

Still he just couldn't stop the sweets. He supposed one day he would. He supposed when he got a girlfriend, although the concept of losing some timber to get a girlfriend hurt his head, which was why he retired into the wonderful heads of others. Whilst other kids liked to play 'Fortnite' or watch YouTube videos of Logan Paul, Roger liked to get lost in his books.

And here was the perfect place to do that. In front of him was the crematorium and graves but behind him over a wooden fence there lay a deep emerald green field filled with horses. He liked horses. Wouldn't ride one, but he liked to admire them from afar.

He liked the smell of the flowers on the summer breeze, although he'd have never dared admitted that. Mostly though he liked how the place felt. Like time had stopped. Like that world between worlds C.S. Lewis wrote about in the 'Magicians Nephew'. Roger loved his books and stories. Mostly fantasy stuff like C.S. Lewis and Tolkien but sometimes he would read Stephen King and all the free fantasy horror books that popped up on his kindle.

His kindle was his prized possession. He even gave it a name. Karen. Aptly named after the greatest singer ever, Karen Carpenter. It was the music his mother had introduced him too and he fell in love with it. Then he watched a documentary about Karen and all her problems with Anorexia Nervosa and he promised his mother she would never have to worry about him making himself sick. That night he cried for Karen. Life could be so unfair. After listening to her music for so long he felt like he knew her, and in his head, he thought Karen Carpenter was a lovely soul.

A bigger love than the Carpenters was his books. He had all his favourite stories on his kindle in sections and categories. Every Christmas when relatives would ask what he wanted he would ask for vouchers. Then he'd spend a day carefully pondering over which books he wanted to purchase and download. Everyone else in fifth year, or at least the ones that read, always read 'Harry Potter' or 'Game of Thrones' books. They used to read the 'Twilight' stuff but that seemed to have died away. 'Harry Potter' was always in style though, but Roger couldn't read any books he couldn't relate to or that his classmates liked. He knew the whole of his year at Kirby hated him but he also imagined the whole of 'Hogwarts school of Witchcraft and Wizardry' would hate him too if he was a student there. Roger had problems. One was that he thought everyone hated him.

But he liked the old books. They didn't hate or judge. In his opinion, they were better written and of course most were free and when he had zero money he had little choice. He was thankful for this because he'd found a wealth of voices and friends from the past to comfort him.

His favourite all time book was 'The Woman in White' by Wilkie Collins, a superb mystery novel. Plus, it was the only book that made him truly fall in love with a character. Laura Fairlie, he imagined she looked somewhere in between Mrs Davision the sixth form art teacher and Maggie on the TV show 'The Walking Dead.'

*

Today was a good day for Roger. Firstly, Dashers newsagents were selling reduced priced Mars bars, so he bought three. Second, it was easy to get out of school today because his mothers car wouldn't start so he said he'd take the bus. Only he never got off at the school, instead he exited five stops early to come to the Crem.

The walk through the graveyard was

pleasant. No one was around and thankfully there were no funerals going on.

Birds chirped in the sky, the aroma of a bonfire was in the air from somewhere far out of sight and best of all, was the reassuring swing of his blue carrier bag against his thigh as he walked.

If only he had a girlfriend it would make a great day perfect.

He brushed a hand through his thick mop of brownish, red hair and with it swiped away any ideas of girlfriends and the things he'd like to do with them. This was a perfect day for reading. Today he planned to read 'Moby Dick' and gorge on chocolate.

He walked around the graveyard, along the tarmac road towards the crematorium. Suddenly he stopped.

There was a car. Not just any car but a hearse. Roger stared at it for some time. It didn't look like the regular hearses he'd see here. This one looked American; like a Cadillac from the movies. Worse still, it was parked at the back entrance right next to his grassy knoll.

That's my day ruined, thought Roger as he approached the car. Suddenly, the carrier bag of junk felt like a dead weight in his hand.

He walked around the car. No denying

how nice it was; polished to a shining sparkle with wheels bright as silver. Roger stopped and looked through the window. The front one was open a few inches. The leather inside was tanned and looked brand new.

He remembered all the other funeral cars he'd seen here and how normal they looked. Without thinking, he leant down close to the open window and there it was, the smell. That 'fresh car' smell. Gently he ran a finger over the metallic door and…

'Boy!' shouted a bellowing voice.

Roger fell backwards tripping over his own legs like an idiot landing on his ass. His bag opened and a rogue mars bar burst out.

From under the car he saw legs walking around towards him. They wore black trousers and shoes that were so polished they glistened in the sunlight.

Roger got up quickly.

An old man stood staring at him, no wait, he's studying me; looking at me like all the kids in fifth year do.

The stranger was dressed in a grey blazer, crisp white shirt and black tie. His long grey hair was combed back over his balding head. His stare focussed from one wide eye as the other clenched closed, like a menacing Popeye. And well, he was tall and looked heavily strong with huge shovel like hands. Roger didn't plan on running. He doubted he'd get far. Suddenly the tall man walked a step closer and…

'I'm sorry if I scared you son' said the stranger in a warm soft voice, his face relaxing into a smile, just before sticking out his hand.

Roger gasped and the tall stranger smiled; his face looking less angry and scary and more like a kind uncle. Actually, thought Roger, he looks just like Roald Dahl and for a second he imagined the stranger was Willy Wonka.

He shook the strangers hand. It felt strong.

'I've seen you here before haven't I young sir. You sit on the grass reading your thingy. I like to read too, although not on those things. I like old fashioned books.'

'Yeah, I used to like books, then they closed our library.'

The stranger looked distressed at that and held a hand to his mouth.

'That is sad. Everyone should have the opportunity to read and better themselves. If it hadn't been for the adventures of Huckleberry Finn I would have been in all sorts of trouble as a child.'

Roger smiled. He instantly liked the man. Despite his mother telling him never to talk to strangers, he felt he was a pretty good judge of character.

'My name is Roger. I do come here sometimes. Actually, quite a lot. But I don't cause any trouble.'

'Problems at home or school Roger?' asked the stranger gingerly.

'I hate school, far too many reasons that would interest you.'

'So, you come here and get lost in other worlds, eh?' asked the stranger.

Roger shook his head unsure about other worlds until he realised the old man was referring to his books.

'My name is Alistair Crone. I work here and take care of the crematorium, making sure its always clean and nice for people, and sometimes I do what's called a service.'

'My uncle had a service when he died, but I didn't go' said Roger glumly.

'Funerals are no place for children, and I say that from attending so many. When my own father lay dying he made me promise not to go to his funeral and never attend the chapel of rest to see him after he was…' the tall man stopped and nodded knowingly.

'Would you like a glass of lemonade. I have some inside. It was for a family but they just called me to say the funeral has been delayed.'

Roger thought about it and then just as he was about to say yes…

'No, I'm okay, I'm not staying here today. I have to go home.'

The old man's smile faded for a second as he glanced down at the boy's carrier bag. Slowly he bent down and picked up the stray Mars. He studied it in his big hand.

'Oh, I used to love these' he moaned. 'That was before I had diabetes.'

'My mam has that too,' said Roger pathetically.

'We all have our problems, don't we?' said Alistair smiling. 'What matters in life is how we deal with them. I prefer to always try and find the good side in others and always start the day with a smile, and two eggs,' laughed the tall man. 'Anyway I must be getting inside. If you change your mind you are more than welcome. I am always around. But if you prefer to sit on the grass reading your electric book thingy, I won't bother you or get in your way. It is peaceful, here, isn't it?' remarked the tall man, looking around at all the splendour.

And with that he was walking away, around the corner of the crematorium. Roger felt bad because maybe a glass of lemonade wouldn't have hurt. It sure was hot enough for some.

Alistair, the tall man, walked out of sight.

Roger looked back at the great car and then decided to go back to school. Perhaps come back tomorrow.

As he past the car he stopped; he felt a deep remorse. It was nice to talk to Alistair Crone even if it was only briefly. It was nicer to forget he had double maths in the afternoon.

Screw it, he thought and jogged after the stranger.

*

The doors of the crematorium opened with a huge aching yawn. Roger walked inside and as he stepped on the plush blue carpet, that smelt like lavender, he felt slight fear. To his sides were pews, just like a church. The windows were stained glass and deeply set into the walls. At the front was a small alter and a long table. Behind it an even longer table with flower pots and urns. Everything had a weird stillness to it.

'Listen,' said the tall man gently closing the heavy doors.

Roger stopped and did just that. He could hear the warm, all encompassing nothing.

'Best sound in the world. Best sound to exit the great stage eh?' said Alistair and patted Roger on the shoulder before walking in front of him towards the alter.

'Come, I have an office at the back' he mentioned and Roger saw a curtain behind the alter. Suddenly the great wizard of Oz came to mind.

Roger followed the man who pulled back a curtain revealing a single white door.

The office was just as nice. It had magnolia walls with the same blue carpet. There was a desk with a dark green leather sofa against the back wall and near the door was a sink with a few flowers in it. The whole room stunk of flowers, thought Roger and not in a good way.

On the wall was a corkboard filled with post-it notes and leaflets but more interesting was the small painting that hung nearby. It was a beach, but the sky was blazing crimson. Roger thought it looked like hell, if hell was a place. It was perhaps inappropriate for a crematorium, but cool all the same.

There was another door in here; it was black and only half the size of a regular door. Roger would have to duck if they were going to go through that door. Roger saw it and couldn't take his eyes off it or it's brass handle. Around the panels of the door was the thinnest gold lines. It looked strange, like it didn't belong in the room. Before he could ask he noticed Alistair staring at him...

'Nothing, there is nothing through that door boy. Nothing good anyway.'

Roger looked at him puzzled. The warmth had left Alistair Crone's face and it looked like he was studying him. Then like a click of fingers, Crone smiled 'I'm only joking with you son. That's where we keep the cleaning stuff and the vacuum cleaner.'

Roger gasped and the tall man laughed.

Roger laughed too until he noticed the two glasses of Lemonade on Alistair's desk. They had ice cubes in them and beads of cold sweat running down the sides of the glasses.

Roger felt his top lip getting moist.

Where those glasses here when I came in?

Crone smiled and picked up a glass, holding it out for Roger who took it eagerly.

'Please have a seat my friend,' said Crone

as he sat down behind his desk. Roger quickly followed suit and sat on the leather sofa. Then he took a deep drink. It tasted good. The best lemonade he'd ever tasted.

What was the after taste though? Was there an after taste?

Behind Crone two thin windows were open. The morning air felt great, although no doubt it would vanish and be replaced by afternoon humidity. Roger had tried to look in these windows many times when he was outside but it was pointless, the glass was frosted.

'How did you come to be here?' asked Crone before sipping his drink.

What kind of question was that? thought Roger.

'I got the bus.'

Crone smiled and then laughed.

'I'm sorry, I mean how did you come to feel as sad as you are?'

'Sad' repeated Roger, like a parrot.

'I can see it in your eyes, son. Something troubles you.'

Roger looked down into his drink. The ice was starting to melt. When he lifted his head back up he didn't want to tell the tall man about the bullies and being invisible to the opposite sex, but it all just came out. Better still, Alistair listened and didn't mock him. Roger had expected people to laugh when he told them about his insecurities. He expected them to howl like Benjamin McDaniels did when he mentioned how embarrassing PE was because everyone pointed and made jokes about his man tits. He expected Alistair to tell him what every other adult says, 'punch them back, a kid your size would eat them for breakfast' but he didn't.

He listened.

When Roger was finished, Alistair asked if he could speak. Actually asked thought Roger. No one asked him if they could speak; most of the time his mother would just talk over the top of him.

'Do you know what school does?' Alistair said leaning forward 'It gives bullies power. But the biggest thing about school is once you leave, the bullies often find they are nobodies on the outside. The sports stars are merely average and the girls you thought were pretty, are bland. Your world now is school and you hate it, but I promise that won't always be your world Roger.'

'I wish I wasn't fat though, that has nothing to do with school.'

'It won't be forever, I promise. I was just like you as a child.'

'Really' asked Roger unsure.

'We can change when we want to Roger. For example, after I left school I was in the army. I did some terrible things, and I will never tell anyone what I had to do. But, I promised myself, as soon as I left the army I wouldn't hurt a single living thing and I wouldn't ever lose my temper.'

Alistair looked deeply remorseful and Roger wanted to say something kind. Something like Walter Hartright in 'The Woman in White' might say, instead…

'Are you married?' he said.

Alistair smiled and although he was deep in thought he looked happy in whatever those thoughts were.

'I was married once, to the most beautiful lady in the world. Her name was Cathy. When I remember her now, it's the way she looked when we got married. How she sometimes looks when I see her in my dreams.'

Damn thought Roger, wishing he could feel like that about someone.

'I never want to fall in love. I'd hate to lose someone' he said defiantly.

'Nonsense' said Alistair 'to fall in love and share your world, and even your books with someone else is what this life is all about. I had forty-three years with my dear Cathy and losing her was the worst, but I'd have been far worse if I'd never met her.'

Roger looked down at the blue carrier bag full of junk. It didn't seem as appealing now.

'What is your favourite book Alistair' asked Roger. It was a question he asked everyone he was comfortable with.

Crone smiled and thought for a while then clapped his hands together and then shook his head before pointing a finger upwards like the answer had just come to him.

'I like an old book called 'Sense and Sensibility', answered Alistair smiling.

Roger hadn't read that one, but he was sure it was free on his kindle. He also thought it might be a romance book which he didn't like.

'What do you like about it?', Roger asked.

'Well I like the time period and the setting. But overall, I like the story and Dashwood family. It's a story that's like a comfort food to me. Whenever I feel glum I read it and I'm transported away to the Sussex countryside. I used to read Cathy a chapter of that book when she was in the bath and she would do the same for me.'

Roger smiled; it was nice to hear someone so passionate about books.

'What is yours…?' asked Crone and Roger quickly replied

'The Woman in White'

Alistair smiled and clasped his hands together 'You've read the Woman in White, what a marvellous book that is. Wilkie Collins was a fine storyteller.'

Roger was thrilled at the genuine astonishment on Crone's face.

'I like that its like reading peoples diaries' replied Roger.

'Have you read Dracula then?'

Roger shook his head and Crone gasped.

'Oh, you must read Dracula. That book has the same narrative text, it feels like reading a diary, a very scary one.'

'I'll check it out,' said Roger making a mental note, although he wasn't sure about 'Sense and Sensibility.'

Alistair picked up his glass and held it out, 'To good books!' he said and they toasted their book love by clinking glasses together when suddenly, as if waiting until this moment, there was a loud crashing bang in the room behind the small black door. Alistair spilt some of his lemonade down his chin, soaking his shirt.

'What was that' gasped Roger.

'Something fell over!' said Alistair almost shouting.

Roger looked down, scared and unsure. When he looked back Alistair was smiling and in his hand, he held two turquoise balls about the size of golf balls. He rolled them between his finger, as if they were moving themselves to the faint ringing that echoed inside them.'

'What are those?'

'These…' said Crone, his eyes not leaving Rogers 'These are stress balls. They help me to stay calm.'

Roger didn't like the menacing way Alistair was looking at him.

'What was that noise Sir.'

'It's an ancient place. Things have a habit of making noises' said Alistair, staring at Roger, his eyes focused and troubled.

What a strange word to describe a cupboard thought Roger, Ancient.

'I best go now Sir.'

I called him Sir twice just now because I'm scared.

There felt like a shift in the room. It was

still warm, but not as much but…

Suddenly Alistair dropped his stress balls into his blazer pocket and snapped back to reality.

'Of course. I'm sorry I kept you. Please forgive my rudeness.'

He got up and escorted Roger out of the room.

As Roger walked down the aisles of the main room, there was another bang from behind him, in that room, behind the small black door.

Alistair opened the large oak oval door and sunlight stung Rogers eyes.

He stepped back out into the world and turned to face his new friend.

'Sorry, Roger, I didn't mean to scare you. I hope you'll come back tomorrow. It would be nice to have another chat.'

'That would be good' said Roger, and before he could say anymore Alistair was closing the huge door on himself.

Roger looked down.

He'd forgotten his chocolate. Ah who cares, he thought. He didn't feel hungry. Then he remembered his Kindle was in the same bag and felt a sudden despair.

The frosted window is open a voice in his head told him.

Quickly Roger jogged awkwardly around the crematorium to the side of the building and to where the windows were located when he stopped.

There were the windows along from the stained glass ones. But the door, the small, black door from inside the room behind them, where was it? If it was located next to them inside, there was nowhere on the outside it could go to.

A door that opened on a wall?

Roger rushed to window and peered through the crack.

Inside Alistair was standing staring at the small black door.

'I told you not now!' he ordered at someone out of sight and there was another bang. Roger gasped and craned his neck but it was no good. From his position, he could only just see the bottom of the black door which was open. He craned further and tried to tilt his head in the gap, when suddenly a strong hand grabbed his thick hair.

The tall man Alistair Crone was suddenly at the window staring back angrily, his hot breath burning against Roger's face.

'What if I told you all the death and

despair of the world was in here, behind that door! Would you want to see it then?'

Roger give out a cry and the tall man let go. For the second time Roger fell on his ass. Quickly he got up, ignoring the tall man who seemed to be calling for him from the window. That day Roger did something he'd never done in his life… he ran home. When he got there, he puked bile onto the front lawn, but still he'd ran.

*

The next day Roger was eating breakfast wishing he had his kindle for company. The Cheerio's were tasteless – all he could think about was the crematorium and the tall man Alistair Crone. His mind raced with ideas about what was behind the small black door. In his mind he kept picturing it, staring at it over Alistair's shoulder as they sat talking.

It looked like it was painted with the kind of paint you cover metal fences and gates with, he thought.

What is behind that door? Was it like the painting with the red sky? Was it a doorway to another world?

Suddenly he heard his mothers banging footsteps walking across the landing. She shouted something colourful about the car still being broken. Roger shouted back that it was fine and finished his cereal. It was fine too; he didn't plan on getting a lift or the bus. Today he felt like running.

Kirby Graveyard and Crematorium was the same as yesterday. Quiet and warm. Roger thought it might even be warmer as he walked gingerly down from the main entrance to the gloomy crematorium building.

I left my sweets and kindle.

That was his excuse for going back and seeing Alistair. He had to know what was behind that door to. Although it would have been nice he thought, to get his kindle back.

The hearse was outside and as Roger was about to walk around it he saw the figure sitting behind the wheel. It was Alistair Crone. He was wearing a white panama hat. He turned his head and smiled at Roger.

'I wondered if you would come back, young sir?' he said apologetically.

'I was a bit scared,' said Roger his voice cracking slightly.

'Oh, I am sorry, I do have a habit of losing my temper,' he said getting out the car. 'Say you don't believe there is another world behind that silly door, do you?'

'You grabbed my hair.'

'Yes, I took things too far I'm sorry, I do have a tendency for that.' said Alistair

'Sir what really is behind the door?' asked Roger timidly.

The tall man ruffled his hair 'Wouldn't you like to know' he said and winked comically.

'That's okay' said Roger, lying.

'I promise you the truth is far blander than you'd expect'

Roger smiled.

They walked around the building but instead of going inside Alistair directed Roger to the grassy knoll. Roger sighed in relief.

Gently Roger sat down. He wasn't sure but he thought he might have bruised his ass from falling twice the day before. Alistair pulled up his trouser legs slightly and sat down too.

'This is nice here' he said. 'I'm sorry, I say that all the time.'

Suddenly Roger felt bad for trying and wanting to know what was behind the black door. It didn't matter. He'd made a friend in Alistair

Crone. A bit of an odd one, but a friend all the same.

'You didn't want to go to school today?' asked Alistair.

'No, I couldn't face a hot class for geography.'

Alistair laughed, and patted Roger on that knee.

'I don't blame you. If it was up to me I'd sit here all day, instead of in there. Least I remembered my hat today so I don't burn.'

'Do you have a funeral today sir?' asked Roger.

'Yes, but not until two' said Alistair 'and please stop with the sir rubbish. Alistair is fine.'

'Sorry' said Roger.

'Come on let's have some fun' announced Alistair standing up.

'Fun?' asked Roger timidly.

Alistair was staring towards the next field over, and the horses.

'Yes, lets feed the horses.'

Roger gulped, he'd never feed a horse before. But that morning he did. The two of them stood by the crematorium fence overlooking the farmers field. Three horses approached. A white one that was drawn to Roger and two red ones that Alistair petted and fed sugar cubes, he'd pulled magically from his top pocket.

'I ran here Alistair' said Roger feeling good, but aching.

Alistair's eyes lit up, 'And I see you brought no chocolate?'

'I didn't feel like any today.'

Alistair clapped his hands in the air, turned to Roger and put a hand on his should

'I am very proud of you son.'

Roger liked that. It felt a bit dramatic but his mother never said it. No one ever said it.

They continued to feed the horses and Roger talked about getting some better trainers for running. By the time he went home, he'd forgotten all about chocolate and his kindle.

Over the next week Roger missed school everyday, besides Saturday because obviously, there wasn't any school. He went to see Alistair everyday and stayed until three. They talked most morning of books and Roger made a mental note of books to read and even managed to suggest some to Alistair that he hadn't read. In the afternoons Roger would spend his dinner money on sandwiches. Tuna on brown bread was better than he expected and he was getting quite a taste for it. Alistair managed a few bites but didn't seem to have much appetite. Roger thought this was because of the tall man's age. Older people seem to eat less for some reason, although his mother was an exception to the rule. They were world's apart, in age and tastes, but their universal love for books brought them together.

On Thursday, Roger jogged around the crematorium twice, and Alistair timed him using Roger's Casio watch. There was no doubt Roger was getting better at running. He'd ran to meet Alistair everyday and jogged back, in some pain. His muscles were starting to wake up and they screamed at him when they did.

'So, this book, 'The Witches', is a kid's book?' asked Alistair as they sat down on the grassy knoll for lunch.

'Sort of, I guess kids and adults like it. It appeals to both'

'Oh, I must read it' said Crone 'It sounds scary, I can't imagine a writer creating such a book concerning children being kidnapped and aim it at kids.'

'You'll like it, it's a good book.'

'And you will like Sense and Sensibility,' smiled Alistair, to which Roger laughed.

'I'll try it but I hope it's not pompous like those Hugh Grant movies.'

Alistair smiled and stood up, but his smile slowly faded. Gently he took Roger's hand and helped him to his feet.

'It's a deal, I'll read yours and you read mine.'

They shook hands and Roger promised himself he'd read the romance book.

'Roger, I have to go away soon' Alistair said gently, and immediately all the joy of the week was gone.

'What' cried out Roger. 'But why?'

'Ah the crematorium in Furlonger needs a new keeper. Not much business here since they moved burials to High Fell. That's me I'm afraid. Trust me, I'm just as downhearted because I like it here, and I've liked making friends with you.'

Roger could feel tears welling up in his eyes, which he hated himself for. He'd only know Alistair Crone for a little over a week, yet it felt like he was a grandfather or father he'd never had.

'Listen, come back tomorrow Roger, I have a special surprise for you.'

Roger nodded his head. Suddenly, he felt like this might be the last time he saw Alistair and it made him angry.

He walked away without saying goodbye, got a few paces and turned. Alistair was watching him. Roger sighed and walked on.

He walked a few yards and turned again. When he did the tall man was right behind him, Roger grabbed him and held him close. He didn't want to cry but couldn't help it. Alistair rubbed the back of his head, told him everything would be alright and promised they'd have fun tomorrow. It didn't feel odd. It should have thought Roger. He never hugged anyone, not even his mother. This was different. It felt as though the tall man really cared for him, and that meant the world to Roger.

Roger walked home. Even if he'd wanted to, he couldn't run. His bones throbbed and his heart felt heavy.

When he got home, he was greeted by the smell of takeaway pizza. He told his mother who was watching an episode of 'Neighbours' that he wanted to lie down for a bit. His mother waved her hand in the air to be quiet and Roger walked upstairs to his room.

He lay down on his bed and it felt good to rest his legs.

It wasn't fair that his best friend was going away but…

Quickly he sat up in the bed, his head swimming from getting up to fast. He looked across to his bookshelf and walked towards it. There it was in the middle, a paperback copy of Roald Dahls 'The Witches'. It was the perfect leaving present he thought and pulled it from the shelf.

*

The weather wasn't as good in the morning. Roger told his mother he was leaving for school early. She didn't question him as she was still asleep.

He didn't run to the crematorium but he walked at a fast pace. When he got there, he stopped.

The hearse was gone.

Please don't have gone too, he thought and hurried to the crematorium building. The heavy oval door was open a jar. Roger pushed it open further and stepped inside. His eyes adjusted to the darkness of the room as he walked to the back of it.

He expected the white door to be locked but it was open. He went inside. On the desk, he noticed his blue carrier bag from over a week ago. He suspected the kindle and chocolate were still in it, but he didn't care if the chocolate was gone.

The room was the same as when he'd first seen it, only he was alone. Alistair wasn't here. Suddenly he heard the heavy oval doors at the entrance creaking open.

He was about to shout for Alistair when suddenly he saw the black small door. Against all his understanding, he felt himself walking towards it. Now was his only chance to see what was in it. Now or never. He placed the copy of 'The Witches' on the table, took one of the tiny brass handles on the door and opened it…

Inside were several small shelves. The top one had small boxes on it, filled with cards. The others, they had urns on them; about four in total. Under each urn was a card, and…there it was, ALISTAIR CRONE'S name, printed on an eggshell white card beneath an urn. An inscription beneath the name said 'ALISTAIR, A LOVING HUSBAND AND WONDERFUL TEACHER'

On the same card was a small photo of a young man standing in front of a car, his car, the Herse.

He was a teacher? thought Roger as his body started to shake.

Slowly he held out a hand to touch the urn, when there was a movement behind him.

'Boy, what the hell are you doing here!'

Roger turned fast on his heels. At the doorway was a man in his mid forties wearing scruffy overalls and apron. In one had he held a cluster of dead flowers. He didn't look angry, merely confused.

'I left my bag here,' said Roger quickly snatching his blue carrier bag.

'You can't keep sneaking in here,' said the man, but Roger wasn't listening, he quickly pushed past him and ran from the building.

He shoved open the heavy doors and fell to the tarmac outside.

He wanted to scream to tell someone he had seen a ghost or some sort of phantom. A kind and friendly one but...there was no one to tell. He was alone.

*

That night, confused but focussed on his future, Roger lay on his bed. He was angry his friend could be here one day and vanish the next, but somehow it made chilling sense.

Across the room was his blue carrier.

I'm not eating chocolate.

I won't

Suddenly from the bag there was a small audible beep, his kindle had died the good fight. Although its battery had lasted longer than expected, he must have set it to sleep mode.

He lay in bed for an hour staring at the ceiling, remembering his friend, eating lunch on the grassy knoll, feeding the horses and of course, running.

Slowly with aching limbs Roger got up and walked to blue carrier bag, he opened it with the plan to take his kindle and bin the chocolate when he saw…

The book was on it's side, its pages yellow with dust and time.

Carefully he lifted it from the bag. It was a tattered old copy of 'Sense and Sensibility' by Jane Austen.

The faint watercolour cover was cracked and faded but Roger could make out the two ladies dressed in old clothes, walking by a lake.

Roger smelt the side of it for that old book for the flavour that you can't get from an electronic device.

Gently he opened the first page. It was inscribed in blue ink.

To my friend Roger,

My apologies for leaving so soon. I hope you can forgive me. I had little choice.

I hope you enjoy this special book and that it brings you many happy hours.

Remember when I said we all have our problems? What matters in life is how we deal with them and I think you've already started dealing with yours. Everything moves on Roger, as will your struggles.

Thank you dearly for giving an old soul some comfort as he went on his way.

I'll never forget you

Your friend always

Alistair

Roger didn't cry. He felt happy, Alistair had said goodbye to Rogers world. He'd read the book despite it being a romance. He'd read it and remember his friend. A smile rose up on his face. His legs weren't hurting too much…

It felt the perfect time for a run.

INDISCRETIONS

Flight 619 from Miami kissed the runway at Memphis International around one-twenty on a Thursday afternoon. It was a little before two when April Kincaid emerged from the terminal. A stylish leather attaché case in one hand, a pair of carry-on overnight bags gripped in the other, her purse slung from one shoulder; sporting a south Florida tan. She had dressed casually for the flight in dark clinging slacks (no sign of panty lines), a pale sleeveless blouse, and flat-heeled strappy sandals. Her long and thick mane of glossy black hair; she thought it a much better look for her than her natural chestnut, flipped about her face in the warm breeze.

    She paused on the sidewalk and lifted her face to the sun, loving the way it felt on her skin. Comfortably warm, humidity low; couldn't have asked for a better day. She sighed and looked around, spotting the shuttle that would take her to her rental car. Securing a better grip on her bags, she began picking her way through the milling crowd.

    After only a few steps she looked up, hesitated, then drew to a stop, her pale blue eyes peering at the Memphis skyline in the distance. A sight still as she remembered it. Not that much had ever seemed to change about the city. Toward the end of the time she had spent there as April Scott, she had begun to find the city painfully dreary and stifling. No place for a woman with a college degree and aspirations, who had found herself in the role of a suburban housewife. There were times . . . so many times, when she felt like she was losing her mind. Happy enough to leave that life and the city and her ex-husband behind. Her only regrets were leaving the few close friends she made and the way she had failed to stay in touch with them.

But April wasn't big on regrets. Why bother? A waste of time, for the most part, and usually of things better off left in the past and forgotten.

But memories . . . now that was a different story. She had some good memories of her time in Memphis. As she continued staring at the skyline, one of the better ones—a rather juicy and stirring recollection it was, too—buzzed pleasantly in her head. She had met the man at a party. A party her husband didn't attend, tied up with work, as always. A long time ago, and though she'd had a few stiff drinks—more than a few, to speak the truth, to relax her and kill her inhibitions—she still remembered most of the night clearly.

Most of it, but not all of it. The last hour or so, once she and the man had left the party in his car sometime before midnight, was a little blurry in places. April did remember getting home and finding her husband sound asleep, none the wiser. Everything else she remembered of that night and the man she spent it with . . .

. . . she would never forget it. The man wanted her from the moment he laid eyes on her. Emboldened by the alcohol and the way he kept pressing up against her and the way his hands so unobtrusively kept creeping under her skirt, she finally could resist him no longer, and took him to an empty bedroom. He had fucked her from behind, his pants around his ankles, as she bent over the foot of the bed, her skirt hiked up past her waist. As best she could remember, they had done it twice more at his place before she took a taxi home. She might have left her panties at his place, as she didn't make it home with them and she could never find that pair again.

The experience had served as her wake-up call. The first of many such encounters that ultimately led to her divorce and her leaving Memphis.

Out with the old and stale; in with the new and exciting.

The more she thought about it, the more intense the memory became. There was a feeling of heat, raw and powerful, rushing through her, touching her and caressing her in all the right places. A more arousing venture back to the past than she had anticipated; she finally had to shake her head, dispelling the memory.

No time for this; she had things to do. In town on business, she had phone calls to make, an appointment to confirm; a hotel room and some time under a hot shower waiting for her. As she would be in town overnight, she was also faced with finding an interesting way of spending it. No TV or boring movie for her, either. A couple of ideas were bouncing around in her head, provided she could locate one or possibly all three of her old girlfriends and re-connect with them, if only for one night. She only hoped the numbers she had for them were still good.

There was only a couple of other people on the shuttle. She took a seat in back and fished her cell out of her purse to make the first of her calls. The hardest one first, the one she had been dreading since getting on the plane in Miami. Well, maybe dreading was too strong a word, but still a rotten piece of luck and she wasn't looking forward to the conversation.

Nothing else for it, though. She rolled her eyes as she pulled up the number.

"Scott and Associates," greeted a stiff, efficient female voice.

"Martin Scott, please. This is April Kincaid, from Jacobs and Randolph."

"Yes, Ms. Kincaid. One moment, please."

April studied the nails of her left hand as she waited, deciding they could do with a touchup once she made it to the hotel. She would also have to redo her makeup.

"Well, well, of all people," drawled a deep and not pleased voice in her ear.

"Marty," April said, struggling to control

her voice, "to start with, it wasn't my idea. My firm wanted a face-to-face with you and your people, as you know and agreed to. As my office informed you, my boss had a scheduling conflict, so I'm here in his place to pass on all known facts and other info we have on this pending class-action. End of story, okay?"

"I don't suppose you bothered to mention to him that we have history that could and likely will be a problem with this little liaison?"

"Why would I bother doing that?" April countered, her voice low and much colder than she had intended. "I happen to be Wilson Randolph's executive assistant and I travel all over the south and the east-coast if necessary on his behalf. I'm doing my job, Marty—can you suck it up and do yours? If not, I'll be happy to call Mr. Randolph and strongly advise him that we go with another firm. You might like to know that he listens to me and values my input."

"Your job," her ex-husband said, exhaling the words. "Tell me, how many times did you have to spread your legs to get this job? Hmm? How many fuck and suck sessions did it take?"

Only one fuck and suck session to convince him of my value, but what's that to you? "Listen to me, you asshole, and listen closely," April said, her voice now as hard as steel. An older man a few rows ahead of her turned in his seat and stared back at her, disapproval etched on his face. April ignored him and went on. "If you expect me to grovel at your feet and beg you for forgiveness, you're SOL. I said it then, and I'll say it again—the day you hit me with divorce papers was the biggest favor you ever did for me. I moved on to bigger and better things, and I'm happier now. It happened, Marty, and I'm not sorry for it or that you found out about it, so get over it. As far as who I spread my legs for and how many times, that's none of your damn business."

A long silence in her ear, then, "Still the cold-blooded bitch you turned out to be, I see. You're fucking incredible, April. A real piece of work, you know that?"

"Save the compliments, Marty, because I'm not interested. All I want from you is a time to meet tomorrow—and make it early. I have a plane to catch back to Miami."

"Nine o'clock sharp—and may I suggest that you not go out tonight in search of a stud service and end up late tomorrow morning?"

"Thank you, sir," April drawled mordantly. "I'll see you at nine." She ended the call and blew out a breath. *God, what a dick!* The thought jarred the liberating memory loose in her mind again. It was enough to make her grin; that led to a private giggle she couldn't contain. *I'll say what a dick! God, once he finished working me over with that thing, I was sore for days afterward. More than you—Marty, could ever find time to do for me.* Marty had become so absorbed in his firm . . . along with another reason . . . that he had pulled away from her.

The man seated ahead of her, she noted, was still staring at her. When he opened his mouth, clearly about to voice an opinion, she gave him a withering glare.

"If you're about to enlighten me with your bullshit ideas about the way you think a woman should conduct herself, save it for someone who wants to hear it." She spoke low enough so that only the man could hear.

He closed his mouth and quickly turned his head, eyes forward again.

That taken care of, April looked down at her cell, thinking about the other calls she wanted to make. In the end, she decided to wait until reaching the hotel. Maybe after she had taken a nap. If her old friends were working, that would give them time to make it home. She dropped her cell back into her purse and stared out the shuttle's window, anxious to get going.

Another fifteen minutes passed, and three more passengers boarded the shuttle, before the driver finally began pulling away from the curb. April, still staring out the window, expelled a sigh of relief. She was turning her head to face forward when . . .

. . . someone in the crowd caught her eye. A tall and rather handsome man with dark hair he wore cut short and neat. He had the broad shoulders and thick chest of a body-builder and hardly any waist at all. A cell phone pressed to his ear, the man had spotted her and was staring straight at her, a lopsided smirk lifting one corner of his mouth.

April gasped in surprise. *Kevin? My God, can it really be him?*

An older version of the man she remembered, and he had filled out ever so slightly and now had a trim beard. But it was him . . . Kevin. The first of her—God, how she hated the phrase! —one-night stands. Still, the first who had made her see sense, and had driven her to near-screaming orgasms, the like of which Marty could never do for her and had stopped trying.

Marty had just seemed to lose interest in her after . . . well, after . . .

April refused to let herself dwell on the reason why, her eyes still fixed on the man, and it was Kevin. She would know him anywhere. It was the smirk. No mistaking that. Once they had made it to his place, though this part of it was a bit sketchy in her mind, she remembered looking up at him, locking eyes with him as he laboured on top of her, electrifying every nerve in her body with each hard thrust. That was when she had seen that smirk. She was sure of it.

After that one night, though, she had lost him. Could never find him or re-establish contact with him, and she had tried. Soon after that—all too soon, or so it had seemed—she had lost herself in the world of busy lives and a nasty divorce.

Yet there he was—and he had obviously recognized her, despite the change of hair colour. Then again, that was all that had really changed about her appearance. *I let you get away once, but I'll be damned if I'll make that mistake a second time.* April signalled to him to wait, then gathered up her bags and her purse and was on her feet.

"Stop this thing!" she yelled at the driver, ignoring the surprised faces that turned in her direction. "I need to get off!"

The shuttle stopped with a lurch.

When she reached the man, who had given her such a reproachful stare, she hesitated just long enough to glare at him. "Don't even think about it," she spat, and hurried on.

*

He was waiting for her on the sidewalk. April, excitement rising in her and her whole body feeling warm and flushed, had to force herself to walk slowly toward him, a bright smile on her face. He was still giving her that smirk, and it was giving her almost the same sensations as she had felt the last time she could remember seeing it. She couldn't suppress the feelings that seemed to be rushing straight to her centre.

"Look at you," she murmured. "It's good to see." The beard he sported made him look older and much wiser. She would have preferred him smooth-faced—a sudden, though hazy memory appearing in her mind's eye of his face buried between her legs that made her clamp her thighs together—but it was hardly a deal-breaker. Might even make it better with him than she remembered from the first.

"Good to see you," he said, his eyes dropping and quickly roaming over her. "Talk about a piece of luck."

God, don't I know it. His voice was a little different than she remembered, but it had been four years. Who remembered the exact sound of anyone's voice with the passage of that much time? All that mattered to April was the look in his eyes.

He wanted her, and even more than he had four years ago.

April dropped her gaze, noticed the ring on his finger, and her smiled dimmed ever so slightly, but only for a second. So what? She didn't care. It wasn't her problem. Besides, who was she to make an issue of it? They had a fantastic night four years ago and it was clear that Kevin wasn't the settling down type, despite the white gold on his finger.

"I have a car waiting," she said.

"Too bad you let the shuttle get away," he mused.

"It's not that far and a walk would be nice. Give us a chance to talk."

That smirk again. He reached for her two

overnight bags and said, "Right with you."

They said very little during the walk to her rental, or during the drive into the city to her hotel. As she drove, he stroked her leg through her slacks and played with her hand. No words seemed necessary. They both wanted it, as much if not more than they had before. It seemed to April that too many words would only get in the way.

Once she checked in, she left Kevin in the hotel bar, asking him to order her a rum and cola, while she went up to her room to change. As it was only an overnight, she had brought only two other changes of clothes—one, complete with a pair of high-heeled pumps, she planned to wear to the meeting with Marty. But she had packed a skirt, a rather fetching little number that went with her top. Kevin had so loved her in a skirt before, why disappoint him? She quickly changed into the skirt, deciding to stay with her sandals but that she should put on a pair of panties, as the skirt was a bit short, then checked her look in the bathroom mirror.

Looking good, girl. Now, let's go get things started and get some of that.

She entered the bar, glancing over at the young bartender who, strangely, looked like a young Matt Damon. He watched her gormlessly as she walked by. *Took your breath away, didn't I? You just wish it was you, don't you?*

She found Kevin at the table where she had left him. It was a little dark in that part of the bar, and very cosy. He had a rum and cola in hand, one waiting for her on the table. He looked up as she approached, smiled, and nodded approvingly.

"Very nice," he said.

"Thank you." She sat down and crossed legs. Thought about it, remembering how he had stroked her leg in the car, then uncrossed her legs and gently inserted her right foot between his legs. That earned her the smirk again, bringing back the memory and turning on the heat in her again. She felt a finger trailing from her ankle up her leg, then his hand slipping underneath to stroke her calf. His touch felt almost hot enough to scorch her skin. Damn, he smelled good. No, he smelled fucking amazing. All man, and it only fuelled the fire he had started between her legs. She picked up her drink and sipped, then again.

"So, what do you do these days?" she asked, not particularly caring or even interested, merely giving him a chance to finish his drink.

He shrugged. "I'm a dad," he said without emotion. "Mostly I stay home and look after the kids, while the wife works."

April had gone very still. "You what?"

"One of the few days during the week that I have a chance to get out and have a little fun," he added and raised his glass.

Shit, this changed things. *Does this change things? Should he be out fucking around like this when he has a family—like, a proper family at home?* April suddenly felt like asking more questions, but quickly decided against that. Nothing good could come from the knowledge she was likely to gain. She didn't want to know names, and she as hell didn't want to see any photos he might have in his wallet.

Suddenly, the bar and the hotel felt all wrong. And, just as suddenly, the passion—so fiery only moments before—was dying. *Why did I have to ask him that? For that matter, why did I bring him here? Not the place for this sort of thing. My God, there was a family sitting in the lobby, and another getting off the elevator upstairs.*

"Maybe we should take the party somewhere else," he observed, watching her closely, his hand still caressing and stroking her leg.

Even that no longer felt right, and she withdrew her leg from his touch. "Just what I was thinking," she murmured, then took another and longer sip of her drink. "Suggest a place?"

"Yes, I can. A little more removed from downtown and not as swanky as this place." He paused, as if considering his next words, but April didn't give him a chance to say anything else.

"Let's go," she said, picking up her purse and getting to her feet.

The young Matt Damon bartender watched indifferently as she left with Kevin.

*

The DaleStar hotel, near the south end of Beale Street and several blocks over, was two stories, cheap, but not a dump. Not quite, anyway. It went for a deep red theme that reminded April of that fucked up TV show from the 90's that Marty had so worshiped when they were married. April thought the place could use the touch of a good decorator, but for their purpose? Perfect, and she felt much more comfortable there. The hotel even had a bar.

"Another round," Kevin said, and rather brusquely it seemed to April, and headed that way. "We can take it upstairs with us."

"Good idea," April said, wishing she had finished her drink at the other place. "Another rum and cola for me," she said, angling toward a door marked Ladies' Room. "Give me a few minutes and I'll be right with you."

She entered the Ladies' Room, stopped in front of the cracked mirror over the single sink, and gave herself a hard stare. *Okay, pull it together, or you can kiss Kevin and this whole thing goodbye. Even* **HE** *is beginning to act put off. Not once did he try to reach under my skirt, or even stroke my leg on the way over here. What the hell is wrong with me?*

April frowned at her reflection, then a look

of what could only be pain crossed her face. She quickly looked away from the mirror, refusing to think about it, and suddenly unable to look at herself. *Why think about that shit now?*

She knew the answer. Knew it all too well . . . and that was the whole problem.

It was when he mentioned kids.

"To hell with that," she muttered. She had gotten off that shuttle for one reason, and one reason only: to satisfy the ache between her legs. An ache that always seemed to be there, no matter how many men fucked her. *And that's all it is— fucking! —and all it'll ever be. So take him upstairs and get on with it before he gets tired of this shit.*

April glanced at herself in the mirror one last time and, strangely, the movement of her head made her feel a little unsteady on her feet. They had left her rental car at the other hotel, taking a taxi to the DaleStar, and she had experienced a moment on the ride over of what had seemed like light-headedness. No mystery what was causing it, either.

The little conflict going on inside herself. A rebellion she refused to tolerate. She had willed away that moment in the taxi; she did it again now.

Kevin was waiting outside the Ladies' Room, a tumbler of rum and cola in each hand. He offered one to her; she took it, a sly and lascivious smile dancing on her lips, and moved closer to him. Her hand dropped to his crotch.

"Think it's time we got this party started, don't you?" she purred, her hand rubbing and squeezing him through his jeans.

There was that smirk again, and it was even more to her liking this time.

"Now you're talking," he said, his voice now thick and expectant.

April took a long and satisfying drink from her tumbler, her other hand still moving and coaxing, her eyes never leaving his.

They started for the stairs. On the way up, much to April's delight, Kevin slipped his hand under her skirt. She favoured him with her best *'go for it'* smile. He took the hint, gently caressing the mounds of her ass like two pieces of exquisite pottery. On the landing between floors, he stopped her and wedged her into a corner, his hand now slipping under her panties and into her wetness. April expelled a long, shuddering breath.

"You better hurry and get me to that room," she breathed.

At the door, she spilled a bit of her drink as she fumbled with the key he had given her. The DaleStar didn't do fobs. Stuck somewhere in the 80's, perhaps even further back than that. As she finally got the key inserted, she noticed a man with a huge gut at the end of the red walled corridor. He stood with arms folded, a cigarette drooping from one corner of his mouth. He was watching them with small, beady eyes.

It was at that moment that Kevin flipped up her skirt, giving the fat man a view of her ass and her thong panties. Kevin leaned close, his lips at her ear.

"Bet he'd like to bite that," he whispered.

April giggled, a slutty tittering. "Bet he would, too," she whispered, turning the key. As the lock's tumblers clicked, she heard a door slam. She looked and discovered that the fat man apparently wasn't interested after all. "How about that?" she said to Kevin, pushing the door to their room open. "Guess he doesn't like women."

*

The room was small, with a King-sized bed (as Kevin requested), and an adjoining room with a small bath and sink. Two long dressing tables were at either end of the bed, on top of one a pair of tumblers, an ice bucket, several bottles of spring water, and a small assortment of liquor miniatures. April looked over the bedspread, noting there seemed to be no threadbare spots or cigarette burns. Directly across from the bed two large netted windows blazed sunlight.

"Not much of a minibar," Kevin observed, surveying the array on the dressing table. He sounded a little disgusted. "Only been here one other time. Guess I should've suggested where I usually go, but this one was closer."

"Oh?" April arched her eyebrows. "And

where is it you usually take your ladies, Kevin? The Ritz?" She giggled, then drank from her tumbler. It was almost empty. As she lowered the glass, her head seemed to swim again slightly. It was then that she remembered that she had eaten virtually nothing since the night before in Miami. *The rum's going straight to my head. Well, what the hell? Not like it's the first time.*

Kevin had turned away from the dressing table, now giving her a look in reply to her flippant question. A look that could have implied any one of several things, none of which April cared for. He said nothing as he started toward the window, unbuttoning his shirt.

"Careful someone doesn't see you," April teased.

Kevin flashed her another look over his shoulder; April liked this one the least of all. He tossed his shirt on a chair near the window and began working at the snap and zipper of his jeans. April watched him, a hungry glint in her eyes, as he pulled off his boots and socks, then his jeans, leaving him in only a very tight pair of colourful briefs, and those didn't stay on very long.

But something was wrong. The way he had undressed seemed so . . . formal. Where had the passion gone? That raw desire and urgency he had shown on the stairs?

And why did she still feel a little dizzy? It was like being under water with her eyes open.

She could also feel the beginning of a headache. *Oh, this is just fucking wonderful!* She sensed more than saw that Kevin had turned from the window and now stood facing her. She could feel his eyes on her. She forced her eyes to focus, wanting to again see and to savour the sight of his enormous package.

Suddenly, the room seemed to shift to one side; April felt like she was losing her balance. Then she sensed Kevin's presence beside her and felt a hand gripping her arm to steady her. Her drink, what remained of it, left her hand. April couldn't understand what was happening. *I've had a lot more to drink many times before this and never felt* **this** *way.*

Then, as Kevin guided her toward the bed, she heard her cell phone ringing in her purse. It seemed to break her clouded state of mind for the moment, her eyes again focusing. April pulled her arm from Kevin's grip, located her purse on the bed, and fumbled her cell out of it. She frowned at the screen. A local number, one she felt reasonably sure she knew, but damned if she couldn't remember who it belonged to.

"Ignore it," Kevin muttered. He had moved away from her and was now glancing at his pile of clothes. He went to his jeans and fished his own cell out of a pocket. April watched him, disapproval working itself into her features, her cell still ringing in her hand.

Checking your phone now? Making sure you have

no messages from the wife before you fuck me? April grimaced and answered her call.

"Hello?"

"April?" said a voice she recognized immediately. Jenny Scott—unless she was married now. Marty's kid sister. April had always had a soft spot for the young woman; it had saddened her when she left their friendship behind. Felt even worse whenever she allowed herself to think what Marty might have said about her to Jenny. *Marty probably told her I was coming, and now I bet she's looking for a night out.* Because of the conflict that had, no doubt, arisen from the divorce, Jenny wasn't one of those who April had intended to call when she got off the plane and had completely forgotten about. *Sorry, Jen, but I can't deal with this kind of disappointment right now. Damn, I do hope you're not binge eating again.*

"Hi, Jen. Hey, hang on a sec," April said, rising to her feet. She went into the bathroom, surprised by how unsteady she was on her feet. She closed the door and locked it. The stark white of the bathroom's interior seemed to worsen her blooming headache.

Christ, only two drinks! She sat down on the toilet seat. "Okay, Jen, I'm back."

A pregnant pause, then, "***April***," Jenny gasped.

April blinked. *God, she's crying!* April, sure this was the final blow to her plans, felt her headache amp up a notch. "Jenny, sweetheart, what's the matter?"

"It's Marty," Jenny moaned. "He's been in an accident . . . and it's bad. Real bad."

It felt like to April that her stomach had flipped. All the slutty thoughts that had occupied her mind vanished, the professional woman in her kicking in. "Jenny, tell me what happened."

"All I know is that the police showed up where I work and said he crashed his car about an hour ago. Then . . ." The words abruptly stopped, the woman's voice breaking in fresh sobs.

"Calm, Jenny," April soothed. "Calm down and tell me what you know."

"I called the hospital and they said he was in surgery and probably would be for hours. Then, as soon as I got here, they tell me it's a head injury and that, even if he lives, they'll probably have to induce a coma. Oh, God, April!"

April's eyes had gone as huge as golf balls. *Surgery for hours? Head injury? Even if he lives? Induced coma? Fuck me!* She had always felt that she had come to hate Marty and all the bad things he reminded her of . . . but she never **hated** him. Not like that. Her free hand, as if of its own accord, touched her face. *Marty never liked it when I wore this much makeup.* April quickly shoved the thought and the shock aside. "Where are you, Jenny? What hospital?"

"Are you coming?" Jenny asked the question is if she couldn't quite believe it.

"I'm in Memphis right now. I was supposed to meet with Marty tomorrow about work– and, yes, I'm coming."

Jenny sobbed out the name of the hospital. One of the big ones in downtown; not far away. April told Jenny she was on her way, then stabbed the end key on her phone. *Christ . . . what was the last thing I said to him on the phone?* She couldn't remember, but he had sounded angry—but, fuck, he had always sounded angry!

No, April corrected herself. *No, not angry. Marty was never angry. Never . . .*

She suddenly noticed herself in the mirror attached to the back of the bathroom door. The black hair, the makeup; the top that showed off her cleavage, the short skirt. April's eyes narrowed, an eerie sense of horror creeping through her. *My God . . . I look like a whore—some cheap slut that guys find and pick up in bars. When did this happen to me?*

And why is it that you think of the good times, the moments you never want to forget, only when someone is deathly sick or hurt?

*

Marty Scott was such a kind and sweet man when they met. Ambitious, yes, a man going places. Yet he was so down to earth, and anything could please him. Anything at all. Like the picnics they had enjoyed together at Mudd Island along the Mississippi. Back when money was tight, and the food consisted of peanut butter and jelly sandwiches and cans of diet soda. They used to sit there for hours, watching the river and the tugboats pushing their laden barges and the occasional old paddle-wheel steamer chugging past. All those days they had spent there . . . and all of it so beautiful. It had always felt so . . . right to April.

Was it one of those days she had decided that she loved Marty?

Christ . . . maybe it was.

A sudden flood of memories inundated April's mind. Of good times, special times, and all of it before the hurt and recriminations. Painting their first home together, laughing like kids at the silliest things; having the time of their lives. She suddenly remembered the smell of fresh paint . . . of she and Marty making love on the kitchen floor. On the kitchen table or the sofa in the living room. In the hallway between the living room and bedroom. Wherever the moment seized them. It wasn't just fucking then. It was never just fucking when two people loved each other. It meant something then.

When did it stop meaning something?

Kids . . .

They started trying for a kid before their marriage and all through their first year as husband

and wife. But as Christmas of that first year rolled into spring, and Easter into summer, nothing had happened. April had some tests done and discovered it wasn't from want or lack of trying. There would be no kids for them. April was unable to conceive.

Just one of those things.

April had felt broken inside. Pathetic and worthless. As bad as it was for her, it had gutted Marty. He tried to shrug it off, claiming it wasn't that big a thing, but April could look at him and see the truth . . . and how she resented him for it. He wasn't the one who couldn't have a baby! That was her curse, and she needed Marty to be a man about it. To be her rock.

But it had cut him as deeply as her, and he was bleeding inside even more than she.

It had all gone straight to hell from there. She began thinking Marty would be better off with someone else. A normal, healthy woman . . . not some dried up gourd like her. She would get mad at him over the stupidest things and call him such horrible, awful names. Inside, and for reasons she could never quite grasp, she wanted him angry at her. Wanted him to punish her for failing him. But Marty, being the man he was, never so much as raised his voice to her.

Damn his ass!

Their sex life came to an abrupt and crashing halt, and she couldn't deal with that.

There seemed no point to anything anymore. Nothing mattered. Love making? What a fucking joke! What the hell was that when there would be no child because of it? April still couldn't say when the drinking started, and Marty had always acted as if he didn't notice it at all.

Then came all the sneaking around and the cheating. Kevin was the first, but it didn't stop with him. Nameless and faceless men, one after another, a long string of one-night stands. They always got her off, but it never sated that ache in her. Never made her feel like a complete woman. Stuck in a sort of limbo; growing more desperate for that ache in her to go away.

Then the night her marriage died without even a gasp. April, more than a little tipsy and thinking Marty was working late, brought her latest one-night stand home. Marty had appeared from the bedroom, still half-asleep, and found her in nothing but her bra and panties, on her knees and sucking on the guy right there in the living room. She stopped what she was doing and looked at Marty indifferently. The look on his face she would never forget. He wasn't one of the nameless and faceless. He was her husband, and she had just destroyed him. Still on her knees, the guys dick still in her hand, she watched it happen.

And the cruellest fucking thing of all about it was what she had said.

"It's not like we have kids, is it, Marty? So what difference does it make?"

Something like anger appeared in Marty's eyes. Finally, he was going to get angry and yell at her. Tell her what a no-good whoring slut she was. Maybe even slap the piss out of her and run the man with her right out of the house.

Instead, her husband started crying. Great, heaving sobs as the faceless, nameless man with her went limp in her hand. She remembered thinking, *Well, I'll just be goddamned.*

*

Her head pounding and her mind roiling in turmoil, April stood up unsteadily from the toilet seat and stepped gingerly to the sink. She turned on the cold-water tap. *What the fuck have I let myself become? The cold-hearted bitch Marty called me on the phone? My God, if only I could say it stopped there.* Busy with a career she had fucked to get, on a plane and acting the part of a consummate professional most of the time; the rest of the time acting like a good-time girl with any willing man whose dick she could get between her legs.

The worst of it was that she couldn't remember all the nameless and faceless men she had fucked and sucked in her search for what none of them could ever give her.

She watched the sink filling with water; once it was full enough, she thrust her face in the water and screamed. It seemed to take a long time before the moment passed. When it did, finally, she raised her head and she felt a little more in control. She still had the headache and feeling even more woozy, but more like herself.

Like her real self -- the woman she used to be. She grabbed a towel and began pawing at the makeup on her face.

God, I've been so stupid. All the men and the sex . . . and all I really did was throw away the one man that truly cared about me. Marty had told her, shortly after the devastating news of no kids, that he wanted her and no other; that kids were a bonus. April didn't believe him; she knew how much he wanted kids. *Still, you damned slut, he chose you and tried his best to stay with you and to love you . . . until I left him no other choice but to end it.*

A sudden shout from the other room.

Oh, God . . . Kevin. Well, he'll just have to swallow his pride and leave here with his tail between his legs. She had to get to the hospital and Marty. She had to see him, perhaps even talk to him. Even if he somehow heard her words – even if it was for the last time, or if he had even made it this far – it probably wouldn't mean that much to him. Quite possibly all for naught. But she, nonetheless, had to try. To try and tell him that she was sorry, and no longer the cold-hearted bitch that had possessed her for so long. That she had finally woke up.

April drew in a breath, hoping it would ease her headache and the woozy feeling, and opened the door. Kevin stood just beyond the doorway, naked and deflated, his arms folded. No sign of the smirk now, only a petulant glower on his face.

"Are we going to fuck or what?" he demanded as if it had now become a chore, and one he wanted to have done with.

April looked past him, willing her eyes to focus. There, on one of the dressing tables, was what looked like his phone. Lying on its edge, propped against one of the empty tumblers, and pivoted so it pointed at the bed. April scowled.

"You were planning to record us?"

Kevin nodded, a rather strange and eerie light now burning in his eyes. "I like to preserve the moment," he drawled. "I've also found that the footage can come in handy if the pussy wants to object or cause a problem afterward. Especially some professional twat like you looking for a cheap fuck. One word, it goes viral, and I mean everywhere."

"Hate to disappoint you, Kevin," April snapped. "But no pussy or footage for you."

"What, got a problem with it? Must say, I never took *you* for a prude."

"Damn it, Kevin, don't you get it? I have to get to my husband . . . my ex-husband." Without waiting for a reply or even giving him a chance to offer one, April grabbed her purse and was heading for the door. *Damn, all my other clothes*

105

are at my hotel. Will have to stop by there. I can't go to that hospital dressed like this. I could also do with a little coffee. Jesus, why is my head spinning like this?

"Listen, cunt, before you just waltz away," Kevin began, his voice hard and flat, but April whirled around, cutting off the rest of what he intended to say.

"I don't care for that word, Kevin," she snapped. The sudden turn around had left her head spinning even harder. She was fumbling for the door handle, but she couldn't find it.

She saw him coming. Saw the angry twist to his face. But her increasingly fogged mind wouldn't let her react in time. There was a loud smack and the entire right side of April's face seemed to explode in pain. She dropped to the floor flat on her butt, her back against the door and her legs splayed in front of her. *What the fuck? That bastard slapped me?*

She raised her now pounding head and looked up at him, but only one eye now seemed to be working right, and then not all that great.

"First of all," he growled at her, "stop calling me Kevin, you stupid cunt. I don't know Kevin—couldn't care less who the fuck it is."

The words jarred April almost as hard as the slap. One hand to her burning cheek—it felt like someone had rubbed it with acid—she squinted up at the man through her one working eye. *Not Kevin?* No, she realized, the knowledge beginning to seep into her consciousness, it wasn't Kevin. Then again . . . had there ever really been a Kevin? There had been a man she met at that party and she had gladly, drunkenly let him have his way with her, and more than once—that much she remembered. But had Kevin been his name? Had he even mentioned his name? Or was it merely a name that had come to her and she had attached to him and what of the memory had stayed with her? An idea, perhaps even a forlorn hope born from out of the depths of her shattered life and emotions? Another myth of her infertility? Another element of her madness?

Then, when she saw this . . . this stranger staring at her, clearly wanting her, as so many others had wanted her and eagerly fucked her . . . so many nameless, faceless men.

Oh, God, what have I done?

"I thought for sure the shit I put in your drinks would've knocked your ass out by this time, and I could've had my fun in peace," the stranger said, hands on his hips.

*He doped me? The bastard **doped** me? Good Lord . . . how many of the others have done that to me that I can't even remember?*

"Well, no matter—we'll just have to do it the hard way." As if to drive his point home to her, the stranger bent forward, roughly grasping her chin with one hand, and drove his other balled fist into the side of her face.

The blow knocked April to one side, a colourful array of lights dancing before her eyes. She found herself face down on the room's red carpet, too stunned to move or even blink her one remaining good eye. Before she could draw a breath, rough hands grabbed her by the ankles and she realized he was dragging her. She could hear him giggling like a fiendish little boy.

This is hilarious to him? The disjointed thought had barely crossed her mind when she felt herself lifted from the floor. Heard a vague, far away comment about her being so heavy that left her feeling further humiliated, which only added to the rising fear washing through her. She seemed to drop suddenly and hit what she realized was the bed with a hard bounce. Then he was all over her, ripping away her clothes. Once he had stripped her naked, she felt him part her legs and his fingers poking and stroking her. She began squirming, trying to wiggle away from him.

It was then that he rocked her with a couple of hard slaps. Stars exploded in her head much like a cartoon cat that had taken a whap with a frying pan. She felt herself drifting to and teetering on the edge of consciousness.

But April fought it. Bringing all the strength she could gather, all the will she could muster to the fight, forcing her mind to function. *Can't pass out. Can't . . . pass . . . out.*

"Now let the fun begin." A growling whisper near her ear, his breath hot against her skin, the stink of his sweat rank and cloying. She felt him climb off her and get off the bed.

She was coming back. Her head rolled to one side and she watched him standing at the dressing table, doing something with his phone. *He really is going to record this. How many of the others did the same thing?*

She suddenly frowned. *What is that? Music? My God . . . The Carpenters? What is he doing? Dancing?* He was doing exactly that. Seemed lost in the music, though what he had in mind was hardly something Karen Carpenter would have sang so pleasantly about. This wasn't blue birds singing every time you appear, or anything to do with the angels getting together.

This was some sick ritual, a prelude to rape, and he was going to record it.

Viewer discretion advised.

The stranger twirled, hands in the air, then he was back on the bed, astride of her chest. His long but still flaccid cock dangled in her face. He had lowered his weight on to her, as if trying to crush the breath from her lungs.

Isn't this how that sick fuck Gacy killed his victims? By suffocation?

"Come on, cunt," he said, slapping at her face with his cock. "Open your mouth and make your daddy feel good."

"You really don't want me to open my mouth," April hissed, her teeth clamped together.

"Oh, like that, is it? Just for that, you cunt, when I'm through fucking you—and I mean both holes—I'm going to bite your pussy. Think I'm going to bite a piece of it off and swallow it. That way, we'll always be together."

Then he laughed, high-pitched and inanely. The sound of it rendered April cold from head to foot; she had no doubt he would do what he had said. All of it. She had to do something before this fucker was ready to start on her in earnest. She glanced at the dressing table; at the tumbler holding up his phone. *If I could just somehow get to that glass . . .*

But pinned to the bed as she was, it might as well have been a million miles away.

Then he climbed off her, his hand reaching for her, and he flipped her with surprising ease face down in the bed. "Got to get you in the right position," he said, roughly pulling her by the hips to one side. "Don't want to miss getting a second of the action, you know."

April felt herself drifting again toward the edge. Whatever he had given her in her drinks was taking full effect now. That and her pounding head and the pain he had so far inflicted upon her were fast draining her of what little she had left with which to fight him. She raised her face from the bed and stared again at the tumbler on the dressing table. She had to get to that tumbler, the crazy notion that had first come to her again dancing her head.

But what other choice did she have? Something drastic was all that would save her.

Then she became aware of something. The stranger was now breathing hard, mumbling to himself, and the bed was moving slightly. It hit April suddenly what he was doing and what was happening. It might have even been funny if not for the situation. Yet the full absurdity of it was more than she could ignore, and she couldn't contain the tiny laugh that rolled up from her throat and out of her mouth.

All sound and movement from him stopped cold. "You laughing at me, you cunt?"

"Awww, I wouldn't suck you, and now you can't get it up, dickhead? Now I see why you want to bite my pussy—it's all you're good for, isn't it?" A dangerous thing she was doing, but desperation called for drastic measures.

He was suddenly pounding her again with his fists, hitting her back and the back of her head. She rolled to one side and onto her back. Spewing profanities and making little animal-like growling sounds, he kept on hitting and hitting her. April took the blows, willing herself– begging herself— to hold on . . . hold on. She felt something let go in her side, a sharp, stabbing pain stealing her breath. *Hold on, damn it to hell, hold on! He can't keep it up much longer!*

Sure enough, he was quickly gasping for breath, his punches slowing and falling with less and less effect. Her chance at hand, April let her body go slack, as if she had passed out. His punches abruptly stopped, and he rolled off her and lay beside her, panting like an old steam locomotive.

The tumbler . . . one chance to get it.

April rolled off the bed, a searing shard of pain ripping through her injured side, her head and the room suddenly spinning out of control. She scrambled on her knees to the dressing table, knocked aside the phone and grabbed for the tumbler. Her fingers closed around it—*yes!*—then slowly, slowly and painfully, pulled herself to her feet and turned to face the fucker.

He had sat up in bed and moved to the foot of it; still breathing hard, he sat there watching her, a look of pure contempt on his face. "That's a tumbler, you stupid cunt. Even if you break it, which I doubt you can do, you'll never stab me with the pieces."

April, leaning against the dressing table, gave him the finger and laughed. She saw the look that crossed his face and knew he had heard and recognized the lunacy and desperation in her laugh.

But he reacted too slowly to stop her.

She raised the tumbler and threw it, as hard and straight as she could, straight at one of the windows. The glass behind the netted curtain cracked but didn't break.

"Now what was the point of that, you stupid cunt?" he asked, but he was on his feet and already coming for her.

He was only inches away from her when she grabbed him and wrapped her arms around him. He found that funny and laughed, and was still laughing when April, pushing off with one foot against the corner of the bed, propelled them both toward the window. April held him tighter than she had ever held anyone until they had stumbled and staggered to within only a couple of feet of the window.

He was still laughing when she abruptly let go of him, stopped in her tracks, and shoved him as hard as she could toward the window. His laughter stopped, understanding dawning on his face. He stumbled out of control backward, his arms wind milling, and he hit the window with a terrific crash of shattered glass and disappeared.

The nameless stranger's scream abruptly died as he did when he hit the ground below.

And April, pushed beyond endurance and the effects of the drug and pain at last pulling her under, dropped to her knees, then crumpled to the floor.

After that, there was nothing but the blackest of voids for a long time.

*

It was quiet in the hospital room; April was dozing

in the recliner next to the bed. The sound of a voice speaking her name roused her. Her eyes blinked open and she found Marty, his head swathed in bandages and IV drips in both arms, staring at her as if not quite able to believe what his eyes were telling him.

"They told me you were here," he murmured. "Jenny said you had some trouble and, God Lord, you look it. What happened to you?"

April had rose slowly, gingerly to her feet, her broken ribs only complaining a little. She wasn't wearing any makeup, her face a veritable checkerboard of purple and black. Beneath her modest blouse it was even worse. She leaned over Marty and lightly kissed his cheek. "Like Jenny said, a little trouble, but it's nothing for you to worry about. I'm fine and the important thing is you are too, and you're going to make it."

"April," he said, his face growing serious and pained "I thought . . ." He seemed unable to get the words out.

April forced an earnest, contrite smile. "I'm sorry for how unhappy I made you Marty."

"I was never unhappy" he said, his eyes and voice puzzled.

April hesitated, choosing her words. "Marty," she began, "all the days I've been here, there's something I've said to you a hundred times or more, hoping you could hear me, and now that you're awake ... I'm not sure how to say it."

Marty, despite his condition, smiled. A smile that shone, and it made April reach out and take his hand. His smile widened at her touch, and he did something she didn't expect.

He pulled her hand to his mouth and kissed it.

April took a deep breath and averted her eyes. "I've been remembering things, Marty. Remembering those days before things went wrong. Remembering how much we loved each other. Remember the days when we had nothing but the clothes on our backs, a rat-infested apartment, and each other? I remember, and I miss those days. I've missed us." Now she looked at him, locking eyes with him. "Remember?"

"I never forgot," he whispered, his voice making a dry, clicking sound. He was holding her hand even tighter.

April sat down on the side of the bed. They said nothing more to each other; within a couple of minutes Marty had drifted back to sleep. April remained sitting on the bed, watching him sleep, her fingers still laced with his.

THE HAUNTED ONES

How did I end up with such a loser? was the first thought that went through her mind when she saw the old buildings squatting like monoliths in the waning twilight.

Hardly an original thought; Carla Birkley had been asking herself that question for quite some time. As the car drew to a stop near one of the ageing structures, her hand, as if of its own accord, dropped to her belly and she remembered the other man in her life. The one still growing inside her.

Still, Carla wondered, how the fuck she could have ever let herself get with a man like Harold. Even his name was enough to bore her to tears. Yet Harold had saved her; that much she couldn't deny, even to herself. He had literally caught her as she neared rock bottom, snatching her from certain death from an insatiable love she once had of the bottle, and the oblivion the alcohol afforded her.

Carla had tried—only she and God knew how hard she had tried—but no matter how many pretty things Harold had lavished upon her and despite the way he had made a far better life for her than the one she had, she couldn't bring herself to love him. She felt absolutely nothing for him, emotionally dead inside.

It wasn't that he was an ugly man or a slob—far from it, in fact, on both counts—and he was fantastic in bed. He could make her come and come—like she never had before! —with infinite ease. But that was just fucking and that was the easy part. She had spread her legs for one man or another all her adult life and had never felt a thing for any of them. She had hoped—had prayed—that it would be different with Harold…but it wasn't. There just simply wasn't any spark. The torch was out—if it had ever shone at all—and every time they had a fight and she could feel herself drawing closer to the point of telling him the truth…

…he would always remind her that he had been there for her when no one else was. That he was the one who had picked her up after her family had given up on her and refused to even speak to her. The one who was there for her every hour of the day to comfort her and hold her hair back when she vomited.

She could no more deny his love and devotion to her than she could her own lack of feelings for him, and she had always hoped that what he felt would be enough for both of them.

It wasn't, and she could no longer hide from the fact that it never would be.

Another fact she couldn't hide from was that she was pregnant with his child, his son, and she not only hated the idea of raising the child alone, but it frightened her to the depths of her soul. Her own mother had raised six kids alone and ended up dead at forty-eight. She didn't want to be that woman. Still…

Don't be daft, you silly woman. For all his drawbacks and despite the way you feel about him, he looks after you, waits on you hand and foot, and he takes you places…

…like this old primary school, for the love of God!

How fucked up was this? She was out of the car and dutifully following her husband toward an old and abandoned primary school as darkness approached!

God, give me the strength…

*

Carla glowered at Harold. Even in the near darkness of the old musty building, the man should have sensed her unease and realized she wanted to leave the place. Yet, at the moment, her idiot-brained husband seemed more in-tune with the old school on Brunton Street that he was with her. She knew it would take more than her misgivings to make him leave.

A sense of timelessness seemed to haunt Carla as she stared down the long and shadow choked corridor stretching like a cave before her. She could imagine those doors flying open; armies of uniformed children racing up and down the corridor to the sound of the old school bells, a few of which were still attached above some of the doors. It eerily reminded her of her own school days. Not the torturous days of secondary school, which consisted of near daily bullying and a lecherous chemistry teacher who used to force her to pull up her skirt whenever they were alone in his classroom. It was another time she remembered, a gentler time when she was truly happy. Living with her mother, who still had some good years ahead of her. A time when her brothers and sisters would protect her from the bullies. A time when she would eagerly go to school and enjoy such lovely days under the tutelage of dear old Mrs. Hughes.

If only someone had told her it was all downhill after primary school she might have found her way to the roof and jumped, making a wish to break her neck and die instantly in a broken heap.

Maybe I should lure Harold to the roof of this place and push him off. I could always claim it was an accident and collect the insurance…for all the good that would do.

Harold brushed aside some cobwebs and

pushed open one of the large windows along one side of the corridor, the window so caked with grime that it looked black. Carla could only sigh at his child-like excitement as a line of sweat dripped from his chin onto his already sweaty white polo shirt. A sigh that quickly turned into a disgusted moan. Once Harold had the dirty window fully open, she could see a schoolyard, which still had a bit of the sun, a dying ball of fire swimming in a sea of reds and oranges.

"My God…it's beautiful," he breathed.

Carla pretended not to hear, ignoring the wonder in his voice, something she had achieved with great decorum and control throughout their marriage. She felt a warm breeze stroke her face; smelled the hint of a bonfire wafting in from somewhere else. She had always loved these warm summer evenings. Her favourite time for a relaxing stroll or finding a bit of shade in the park, enjoying a diet lemonade and thumbing through a book or magazine. Then, after darkness had settled, curling up on the sofa and catching something good on the telly.

A feeling to which she was no stranger began welling up in her again as Harold leaned out of the window for a closer look at something he could surely see just fine from where he stood. Another sigh from her quickly turning into a moan.

The way he smiled, the way he whistled the same song whenever he was happy, even the way he cut the fucking grass—everything he did made Carla hate him. Not a thing she could do to drown out the emotion. Over the years Carla had tried several ways to combat the feeling. Once she even tried hypnosis, then demanded her money back when she awoke to find she hated him even more.

Carla watched as the breeze blowing through the window made his polo shirt cling to his body. A still lean and athletic body, resisting time and flab.

"Few have dared to venture inside this place since 1956, Carla. That's the year mentioned in my book…when they all seemed to go to sleep, then disappeared."

Carla nodded, turning her face away, rolling her eyes. How she hated his one and only hobby—outside her, his only real interest. *My God, Harold…some men would get into the habit of stopping off at the pub for a few pints and a chance to brag to other men and tell pussy related lies, mostly. Some would even go so far as to have another woman stashed somewhere, so he could indulge in all manner of kinky sex that he's not getting from the wife. But, no, Harold…not you.* Since selling his interest as co-owner of the King Processed Fruit Factory, he had begun pursuing his interest in earnest, reading book after book from the Hutson Central Library. Everything and anything to do with his one hobby…his bloody damned fascination.

Ghosts.

Some nights, early in their marriage when Harold came home late, Carla would hope he would have a better reason than something to do with the fruit in aisle five, row thirteen at the factory. There were times when she even wished there was another woman and, without hate or jealousy or guilt, she hoped that woman could respect and admire him more than she ever could. Failing that, perhaps the woman could fuck and suck him silly and at least make him happy. No such luck, however. A few nights she even wished the phone would ring and she would hear the news he had died in a car crash on his way home.

His interest in the ethereal had become obsession when he had read a story in a book called *"Is it Fact or is it Fiction."* The book featured accounts based mostly in England and the States, tales of true sightings and occurrences, half-truths and downright lies, and sheer and utterly ridiculous fabrications. Everything from Amityville to Derek Acorah's cases. *"Day of the Sleeping Dead"* was the story that captured Harold's fascination. Carla saw it as nothing more than badly written travel reading, something no sane person would ever take seriously. No different, really, from all the trashy horror movies whose makers claimed were based on true stories.

Harold, however, believed every word of the story. It had snared his interest to the point that it was inevitable that the day would come when he would decide to visit the old school. It hadn't surprise Carla when they turned off the motorway and drove into the town of Brunton. Harold hadn't taken a single wrong turn during the three-hour drive, all the time using his beloved copy of *"Is it Fact or is it Fiction"* as others would use a roadmap.

From the window Carla could see Harold's red Jeep Cherokee, sitting parked and dormant on the edge of the grassy field of Brunton School beyond the schoolyard. She was so turned around because of Harold's wandering the old school that the sight of the Jeep surprised her. On a straight line from the window at which they stood, the Jeep didn't look that far away. Yet even as Carla stared at it, wishing she had never left it, it felt to her as if the vehicle was miles and miles away…

…the distance somehow…distorting? *Can that be right? Something's screwing around with my depth perception?* Carla felt a little chill bloom in her belly.

"I feel close to tears just thinking about this place and all those poor children."

"God, give it a rest, would you, Harold? It's not fucking Graceland."

"Think about it, Carla," he went on in an awed voice as if she hadn't spoken a word. "How can it be that all those children and teachers were standing out there in the yard one minute, then just suddenly dropped into a sleep from which they could and would never awake? But, more than that, before any of the other teachers who saw them and what happened could reach them…they were all gone. Vanished if they had never existed. It leaves me shocked just thinking about it and wondering what happened to them and why they disappeared like that."

"What shocks me even more, Harold, is that we're standing in a derelict old school building, which we broke into as the fucking sun goes down."

Harold turned away from the window and gave her his lost puppy expression. He had used it before; on most occasions Carla quickly relented and let him have his way so he would stop it. She wasn't going to give in this time; she could take no more of this and his nonsense. Both Harold and the old building were grinding her down; beginning to make her feel faintly sick.

"Harold," she went in a cold and unforgiving voice, "we've broken into a school that has laid abandoned for years. No doubt these old buildings aren't safe just from the years of neglect. You've brought your pregnant wife to a dangerous place. What if a section of this ceiling should finally let go and fall on us?" She went silent and put a hand to her belly, wincing in surprise as she felt a kick. Not the first time little Harold had kicked, and it wasn't his usual tiny kick, either. There was some force behind this one like the little bugger was angry with her and trying to get her attention.

Harold saw her wince and swallowed, his eyes bulging a bit and his face going a little pale in the growing darkness.

At first, the news of her pregnancy had scared Harold. She told him in late-February in the middle of a long night in front of the telly as they watched a *Breaking Bad* marathon. She recalled vividly how he had dropped his soft drink, spilling it all over the book lying open on his lap. He had just stared at her in wide-eyed and open-mouthed surprise and shock; it had taken weeks before he could finally acclimatise himself to the news. While Harold was now used to the idea, she had learned the quickest and easiest way to shut him up or get his attention was to simply place a hand on her belly. Worked every time…

…as it did now. But the kick had surprised her—it had even hurt a little—and she was still angry and miserable and far from ready to let him off the hook yet.

"I just hope this child doesn't turn out to be a failure like his father," she snapped. The words had seemed to come of their own accord and more out of her misery and the force of the kick than from any genuine desire to hurt him…but hurt him she did. She knew it by the way he recoiled as if she had slapped him. She couldn't believe the words that had come from her mouth.

But it felt good to say it—to finally say what she thought and had feared from the time she realized she was pregnant. It also made her feel something else she hadn't felt in a very long time.

Exhilarated.

But that feeling quickly evaporated as the baby gave her another kick, this one slightly above her navel and a bit harder than the first one. "Ouch," Carla winced, one hand rubbing her belly. "Watch it, you little devil."

There was no reaction from Harold this time. When she looked up, she saw that he had moved away from the window and his lips had formed into a pained and drooping line that made him look much older than his years. In that expression she saw all the times life had cheated him; all the times he had felt lost and worthless. His mouth was now trembling; he wiped away the sweat—or, perhaps, tears, she wasn't sure which in the dim light—from his eyes and sighed heavily.

"Let's go, then," he muttered, walking away from the window.

Before Carla could even ask if he was going to close the window, he was gone, leaving her with a defeated look that lingered in her mind. In that look she again saw the failure he was. The kid who never made the football team; the teenager who watched as the popular boys kissed the pretty girls he could only dream about. The man who lived the lives of characters in books rather than a life of his own. It had left his few friends stunned when he hooked up with her. A drunken lush, for the love of God? But quiet and meek Harold knew what he was doing. Saw his chance, such as it was, given her state at the time. The only real break to ever come his way, and he had grabbed it and run with it. Even though she didn't turn heads as she once had, Harold enjoyed showing her off, which embarrassed her no end.

All the reasons she felt nothing for him and why it scared her to think the baby would turn out to be just like him…another failure. She felt a third kick, again near her stomach, and as hard as the last one. Then, strangely, she felt a trembling sensation inside her as if the baby was…

…laughing?

Quickly, she cleared the corridor to the double doors through which they had entered, pushed her way outside, and hurried after her husband.

He was only a few feet away…but going in the wrong direction. *What the bloody hell?* Another kick, this one hard enough to cause her step to falter. *Why is he heading that way, instead of toward the Jeep? My God…is he leaving me? Leaving me* **here**, *of all places.* The thought crossed her mind to just let him walk away. The keys to the Jeep were in the ignition, so just let him go…

…but that would never do, even as much of a relief as it would be, she had to admit to herself that going it alone scared the hell out of her. Who would take care of her and the house and the bills? How would she know which bank card to use and what day to put out the recycle bin? He took care of everything!

He had stopped walking, now staring at something on the ground. Hurrying to catch up to him, she searched her mind for something remorseful to say—something, anything to make the journey back home a pleasant one. When she reached him, she could tell by his posture that he was all set to play his mind games by only responding to and answering her in grunts. She hated it whenever he ignored her like that and it always made her want to scream.

"I'm sorry…" she began, and deep within she felt like she meant it.

Harold neither moved or responded with even a grunt to her half-finished attempt at an apology. Instead, he was still staring at something as if lost in his own world. She gently linked her hand with his, following his line of sight, but she couldn't tell in the dying daylight what he was gazing at so intently.

"Please, Harold, we can work this out." Still he ignored her, and it irritated her. "Look, stop being so…" Again, she went silent, a puzzled frown creasing her brow; he had started shaking. When she removed her hand from his and stepped away from him, she could see he was shivering from head to foot. "Are you okay?" she asked.

He didn't answer. It seemed as if he wasn't even aware of her. She could smell his sweat mixing with the night air and the hint of a bonfire on the horizon. The only sound from him was the soft expulsions of his rhythmic breathing. *Good God, is he having a heart attack?*

But she quickly realized that he was in no distress; that she had heard him breathe like this—had even seen him shiver this way—before.

Always right before they fucked.

He was excited, for God's sake!

But what the bloody hell had excited him?

It was then that she heard a tiny, even fiendish laugh. A laugh that shattered the heavy silence and made Carla jump in surprise and left her with an inexplicable chill.

It had sounded like that laugh of a child, and it had come from just ahead of where she and

Harold stood. She looked that way, gazing across the schoolyard, and noticed something she had missed before. No more than fifteen, maybe twenty steps in front of them...a black heap lying in the playground, a shadow in a growing pool of shadows. She realized it was what Harold had been staring at all along. Studying it closer, noting the lack of movement from it, she thought it might be the carcass of some dead animal.

That or, more likely, just a pile of discarded rags.

Then she heard the laugh again. The same tiny, fiendish sound...only now it was coming from another direction.

"Harold, is that a kid laughing?" she asked as she felt another kick in her belly. That kick, as hard as the last one and coming when it did just as the laugh was fading to silence, left Carla with yet another inexplicable chill. "I think we should leave," she murmured, one hand to her belly. Then she got another kick, this time more towards her ribs, which made her gasp. "Come on, Harold, let's go. Something's...not right here."

Harold didn't move or make a sound. He had raised his head and it was turning this way and that, as if trying to locate the source of the laugh. Carla tugged at his hand, but he seemed lost as if hypnotised.

"Are you even hearing me?" she

demanded. "We've got to get away from here because there's something...weird going on." She couldn't even venture a guess as to what was happening, but it had spooked her, chilling her to the bone.

Harold, though, seemed as oblivious and entranced as ever. Not knowing what else to do, Carla tugged at his hand harder, almost frantically.

This time she got a reaction...only not the one she had hoped for.

Harold's head stopped moving back and forth, his gaze dropping again to the pile of rags or the animal carcass in front of them. As she watched him in the dying light, a tiny and pleased smile appeared on his lips.

Then she heard another laugh...only this time it wasn't a single childish laugh. It was two, the sounds completely different and coming from different directions.

The chill in Carla turned even colder and seemed to sink deeper.

Without a word or a glance, Harold yanked his hand from her grip and started walking toward whatever it was lying on the ground.

"What are you doing?" she shouted at his back. He walked on and, without another second's hesitation, she ran after him. Before she could reach him, though, both her hands reaching for one of his…

…there was more laughter; this time, it made Carla gasp in fright. It no longer sounded like a couple of amused kids having them on. Now there was a mocking quality to it and it was continuous and seemed to be coming from every direction.

She grabbed for Harold's hand; he pulled free of her grip again, stopped walking, and turned to stare at her blankly, the smile still on his lips.

"Harold," she began, but her voiced failed her when she noticed from the corner of her eye that the pile of rags or whatever seemed to be…

…moving.

No, that can't be! It's got to be the coming darkness playing tricks with my eyes!

The trouble was that she didn't believe it herself.

"Harold," she began again, her voice now shrill, but he waved a dismissive hand in her face, silencing her, then he turned away from her and resumed walking toward…

…and it still seemed to be moving. That, combined with Harold's rather rude dismissal, was all the prompting she needed.

Well, screw you, then. The laughter still ringing in her ears, she turned towards the Jeep and, as best she could in her condition, ran all the way to it.

*

Once inside the Jeep, Carla locked all the doors...but she could still hear the laughter. There was something so...unnatural and malevolent about it, and it seemed to be echoing in her head. She couldn't stop the spell of shaking that seized her.

To make matters even worse, Little Harold was now kicking the living hell out of her, every kick drawing a wince from her. *Sorry to shake you up like that, but mum had no choice about it, so please stop it.* She reached for the key, her shaking hand fumbling with it; finally turned it the right way, the engine roaring to life. When she switched on the headlights, she looked up through the windscreen and froze in place.

What the fuck is he doing?

The way the Jeep's headlights were pointing, Carla could see that Harold was now standing over whatever it was lying on the ground. She could also see the heap on the ground a little better. Enough, anyway, to see that it had shape and substance and likely not a pile of rags after all.

Well, you're welcome to whatever it is, my love. I'll be back for you once I've calmed down…in an hour, maybe two. That should give you a chance to come to your senses again…and am I ever going to give you the very devil for waving your hand in my face like that.

She was about to shift the Jeep into gear when she noticed that Harold had stood up straight and was waving at her. He seemed to be shouting at her, but she couldn't hear him over the sound of the laughter still reverberating in her ears. She leaned over to the passenger side widow, Little Harold still kicking like mad, and wound down the window. Yes, Harold was shouting at her, apparently trying to stop her leaving.

"What?" she called, her voice strained and shrill.

"It's a doll!" she thought she heard him yell back at her.

"It's what?"

"A doll! It's just a ***doll***, Carla! Nothing to get your knickers in a twist about!"

Yeah, my knickers are in a twist—you got that right, asshole! "Then explain the laughing!" she shouted back, the unnatural sound of her own voice only adding to the terror washing through her.

Her last words were barely out of her

mouth when the smell hit her. It was enough to make her gag. It smelled like rotting fruit—much like Harold had smelled many of the nights he used to come home late from work...only it was much worse than that and it seemed to be coming right through the open window.

Harold was still shouting something at her, but she quickly wound up the window ...but it didn't lessen the stench. If anything...it was getting worse.

That was when she realized that the smell was coming from right there in the Jeep. From the backseat...

For a long and agonized moment, she felt paralysed and found that she couldn't breathe. Then, finally, slowly and reluctantly, her eyes drifted to the rear-view mirror.

A small, round face of a girl smiled at her from the backseat, and there was nothing pleasant about the smile. Seven, maybe eight, though it was hard to tell for sure, her teeth black rotted stubs in her mouth. She had long dark hair, the remains of her rotting uniform clinging to her body. Her skin bore the unmistakable pallor of death itself, her face smudged with spots of dirt; her eyes, globes of greyish-white sunk deep in sockets ringed with black, seemed to stare straight inside Carla.

Before Carla could gather the breath to

scream the smile left the dead girl's face and she was lunging for Carla, her tiny hands reaching like claws. The hands—like ice and the skin like leather! —found her neck and latched on to her flesh like leeches, a foul and angry breath puffing into her hair at the back of her head. Carla jerked to one side, one hand frantically reaching for the door handle. She got the door open, was gathering her strength to pull away from the dead girl's grip, when…

…more hands grabbed her. At least two more sets of them from the backseat, one set reaching from the passenger seat, and another—*God, save me!* —from under the driver's seat, the hands gripping her ankles.

With a grunt, as much from fear as effort, she wrenched free of the hands and tumbled out of the jeep and to the ground. She landed in an awkward heap, her forehead smacking the ground. White lights flashed behind her eyes; for a moment, her head swam in a dizzy pirouette and the laughter—louder than ever! —seemed to recede.

The moment passed quickly, her senses returning. She rolled onto her back and stared up at the jeep. There were four lifeless faces that she could see clearly in the Jeep staring back at her, each face bearing a menacingly mischievous smile. *God, don't look at those faces, just get away from them!*

As there seemed only one place to hide, the only option open to her, Carla got to her hands and knees and clawed her way under the Jeep, breaking nails in her scramble to escape. As she was pulling her feet under the Jeep, a pair of hands grabbed each ankle and, with surprising strength and ease, pulled her from under her meagre cover. Too frightened to scream, her heart thundering in her chest and unable to get her breath, Carla felt everything beginning to spin away from her, a creeping blackness filling her mind.

*

When her eyes opened, and her vision cleared, Carla found herself still on the ground with at least a dozen dead children crowding around her. Even though she could still hear the laughter, none of those formed in a circle around her were laughing. They were all staring down at her with the same blank, yet clearly sinister expressions on their lifeless faces. Through their legs she caught sight of Harold, still in the glow from the headlights and again bent over what he had called a doll, though she now doubted if it was really a doll at all.

But that was beside the point. The point was that he seemed absorbed by the doll or whatever and completely oblivious to her plight. Damn the man and damn his bloody fucking obsession! Nor did he seem even remotely aware of the other children now gathered in the schoolyard. They were everywhere—a veritable army of them and they were all laughing. Every fucking one of them, by the sound of it. None of them were watching Harold.

They all seemed to be staring at her...and a few of them were now slowly coming toward her and the others grouped around her.

One of those in the group stepped closer and kicked her in the side. It was like a dream kick; she felt the sharp impact but there was no pain.

"Who are you," she whimpered fearfully, tears now streaming down her face. "What is it you want?"

At the sound of her voice, a hush fell over all the children, their laughter fading to silence as the daylight had faded to darkness. Those marching slowly toward her were still coming, and from out of this horde of the dead a single figure raced forward. A boy, his thick and curly blonde hair lit up in the Jeep's headlights. In the sudden silence, she could hear the pound of his running feet; see the smile that appeared on his face. As he got closer, he began laughing. A screaming and demented kind of laughter.

Carla screamed, and it seemed to jar her body awake; suddenly, there was pain, the spasms rippling through her entire body. She screamed Harold's name as she tried to push up from the ground. Another spasm of pain, the worst yet that made her moan and arch her back. The little bugger who had kicked her had obviously injured her in some way. *Oh, God, no…not that. Please, not that.*

Then the blonde boy was upon her, slamming into her and forcing her to the ground. He screamed manically in her face; she gagged at his putrid breath. He was pummelling her with his heavy feet as if he was gleefully jumping up and down on a bed.

More pain, down below.

Carla screamed in agony; the dead children seemed to take that as their cue and they all began laughing again. Through her pain and above their laughter she heard Harold yelling her name.

But she didn't hear him yelling for very long, her mind again spinning her into the waiting void of darkness.

*

In the darkness, the voices drifted to her as if someone was playing with a volume knob. *"I should've put holes in the top of the jar,"* one boy said to someone. *"I shouldn't have let him die. It was my fault."*

More voices now, fading in and out as if someone was twisting a radio's tuning dial, not letting one station play for too long. Rhymes and songs echoed in and out of her head between bursts of happy laughter and conversation and she wondered...

...she wets the bed, so I don't want her playing with us...

...where am I?

...John Spencer is so handsome. When I grow up I want him to marry me...

...I swear, I saw it, a ghost down by the cemetery pond...

What's happening to me?

...did not. You're such a liar...

...I want to be a dancer when I grow up and wear pretty costumes...

...Miss Musgrove said we're her best class...

Where's Harold, that fucking idiot?

...Tommy's right, you never saw a ghost...

Damn your eyes...right when I need you the most!

*

Carla came awake and found herself in the backseat of the Jeep and it was moving at speed. Darkness had settled fully, the distant moon casting a ghostly light inside the Jeep. Harold was driving; she focused her eyes on the back of his head. As if sensing her gaze, he glanced up into the rear-view mirror.

"You awake, love?" he asked, his voice low and concerned.

"What happened?" Her mouth was dry, her voice raspy, and she was in pain. It seemed that every part of her hurt.

"Can't say for sure. I was looking at the doll I found in the schoolyard, and the next thing I know I hear you scream. I run to the Jeep and I found you sprawled on the ground, out cold."

Carla leaned forward, groaning at a sudden stab of pain low in her belly. She ignored it for the moment and caught her reflection in the rear-view mirror. In the ghostly light that filled the inside of the Jeep she could see a bump as big as a baseball on her forehead. She leaned back in the seat, grimacing at another stab of pain. Turned her head and watched the world passing through her reflection in the window.

"I'm taking you to a hospital, love. Have them check you out."

Oh, god…please tell me it didn't really happen.

But it had happened—she knew it had, all of it just now beginning to come back to her. Suddenly she felt it…

Oh, please no…

She reached between her legs and found her jeans wet and sticky. She withdrew her hand and held her fingers in the pale light.

She was bleeding.

For a long, long moment the knowledge rendered her silent and immobile, a mixture of relief and horror rushing through her. When the moment finally passed, a sense of panic seized her, followed quickly thereafter by a rising tide of hysteria as tears began spilling down her cheeks. She could feel a scream building deep in her throat, but before it could even rip from her mouth…

…she saw the tiny round face that appeared around the edge of the passenger seat. The girl with the long dark hair, the dirty face, and the greyish-white orbs for eyes sunk deep in their sockets. The girl she had seen in the backseat, and she was smiling at her as she had before when Carla first noticed her.

Carla opened her mouth to scream…but nothing came out, her mouth hanging open as if her jaws had come unhinged. The dead girl's smile widened, showing many of her blackened teeth. Her lifeless eyes seemed to glow with the kind of glee that could only come from a child. The girl raised a dirty finger, pressed it to her lips, and sighed a soft, "Sssshhhhhh."

That was when the hysteria won out and Carla finally screamed. A long and shrill scream that caused Harold to jerk in surprise and stomp down on the brake pedal. The Jeep slid and skewed to a stop just off the road; then he was getting out and pulling open the back door; reaching for her.

"Tell me, what's wrong!"

"The baby," she sobbed, both hands pressed to her belly. "It's gone!"

"Yes," Harold said, his voice low and forlorn. He pressed a hand to hers, which were still clutching her belly, and said, "I know it's gone. I knew it when I saw the blood. It must've been when you fell out of the Jeep…you must've hit the ground the wrong way—"

"No!" Carla screeched. "They took it from me!"

"They who?" Harold asked softly, his hands stroking her hair and face, trying to sooth and comfort her, but she was having none of it.

"Them," she declared, pointing at the passenger seat. "The children! All those dead children took the baby."

"What children are you taking about?"

Carla blew out an exasperated sigh. Good God, but the damned man was dense! "All those dead children in that schoolyard! You heard them laughing!"

"I saw no one there," Harold replied, speaking slowly, softly, a frown on his face. "I heard no one laughing. How could I have heard laughing?"

Carla gritted her teeth and, through the pain still racking her body, hissed, "Then how do you explain that?" She was still pointing at the dead girl.

"Explain what?"

"Her, you damned idiot! Are you blind?"

Harold's eyes followed her pointing finger, then he looked back at her, the sad and pitying look on his face enough to make her want to scream again.

"This is where you tell me that it's only a doll?" Carla shouted. No doll could be looking at her and smiling so triumphantly as the dead girl was doing right then. *Fucking evil little bitch…*

"I left the doll lying where I found it, I never took it," Harold said.

Carla stared at him, the horrible realization dawning on her strained and pale face. "You don't smell that awful stench?" she murmured, as much to herself as to Harold. "Like something rotting from the grave?" The smell was the worst it had been; it was all Carla could do to get her breath.

"No," Harold said, then his voice changed, assuming the take charge tone of a worried and badly frightened husband. "You're going through a very bad experience, love, and you're scared. Try not to worry too much—I know that's asking the impossible of you right now, but it's important for you to stay as calm as you can. I'll have you to a hospital shortly."

Then he moved away from her, closed the Jeep's back door, and climbed behind the steering wheel. He never once glanced at the passenger seat.

But Carla never took her eyes from the face still peering at her and smiling. The Jeep was moving again when Carla breathed a soft and shuddering sigh.

So...this is what I get, is it? My punishment for not believing and calling him a failure because he believes? You and the others take my baby away from me...and now, what? I'm stuck with you? Maybe for the rest of my miserable life?

The dead girl's smile broadened and turned insidious. Then she lifted one thin shoulder in a shrug. *So who's the failure now?*

Carla heard the words clearly in her head. Then, as she closed her eyes, trying to blot from her mind both the horrible and leering face and the putrid smell of her, the girl began laughing. A soft and gentle—almost melodic sound—yet wholly mocking in its quality and cruelty. Carla opened her eyes, glancing once at the laughing girl, then at the back of her husband's head.

Harold, of course, heard nothing, his eyes on the road, both hands on the wheel, concentrating on his driving.

Yet the tiny peals of laughter seemed to detonate in Carla's head like claps of thunder. The laughter went on; quickly, it seemed to be robbing Carla of the ability to think rationally, her thoughts turning ugly and deadly. She didn't love the man driving the Jeep—had never loved him…what the bloody hell did she have to live for? Why not simply open the door and tumble out of the speeding jeep to her death?

Seemed better than a lifetime of the dead girl and her maddening laughter.

The laughter abruptly stopped—*won't work, you know. You'll have more than just me to deal with then*—and began again, and it was even more mocking than before.

Carla's head dropped in defeat, her body beginning to heave as emotion seized her and the sobs began. Tears streamed down her dirty and pale face, the dead girl's laughter echoing in her head.

THE LONG DISTANCE CALL

When Alex Coleman got the phone call he thought it was a joke, a sick and pathetic joke.

When the caller rang again and asked him how he was, Alex smashed the phone down so furiously he thought he might have broken it.

He told himself it had been a good impersonation, although he couldn't imagine who would sink low enough to phone him up pretending to be…

When the phone rang a third time he knew it would be best to call the police, but he discovered his rage was too intense.

Quickly he grabbed the phone and was about to erupt into abuse when the voice on the other end told him to calm down.

Suddenly all the obscenities he'd prepared to shout faded away to nothing more than whispers, echoing in the back of his mind.

And that was when he realised this wasn't an impersonation.

It really was his dead mother calling.

*

Alex sat staring into the darkness of his living room. They'd told him the electricity would return sometime that night but still there was nothing. The only thing that worked was the phone, which was still continuing to ring since he'd hung up on…

On your mother, he told himself.

You know that was her voice.

Alex couldn't remember the last time he'd heard her voice. It wasn't when she died four years ago. He knew that because he hadn't been there.

A cold sadness washed over him and he felt that awful churning sensation in his stomach. It wasn't as bad as it had been four years ago, but it still made him wish he could have spoken to her one last time…

And I can he told himself and then quickly dismissed the idea. She'd been dead four years and the person calling him up couldn't be her.

For his own sanity he had to believe it wasn't her.

The phone was one of those old types with a plastic dial wheel you turned to ring, Alex had brought his own when he'd moved into the flat a week ago but when he saw the last resident had left a phone with character, he decided to use that instead, surprising himself when it still worked.

He'd remembered having one similar in his house when he was a kid. It always took ages to ring and was a pain if you got the number wrong and had to start again. Still there was something he liked about the old phones, something that reminded him of better times. There were no lit up caller ID screens with time and date displays that would constantly run out of battery because you always forgot to put it on charge, and neither did it have an annoying ring tone, because it was just a telephone, a telephone that did its purpose without the bullshit. From a simpler time, Alex thought.

The plastic had discoloured on the phone over the years from white to nicotine yellow, especially the curly chord which connected the base to the receiver. That colour was as dark as mustard.

Alex imagined the last owner standing against the wall talking on the phone as they smoked one cigarette after another.

He wondered what kind of person the phone had belonged to and imagined a fat woman with rollers in her hair, shouting into the phone at someone – probably her husband.

There was also something about the ringer's sound. It almost felt urgent, like it might ring so hard that it would knock its receiver from its cradle.

*

Alex stood in the hallway watching the phone ring and after a while he almost fooled himself into thinking the phone was glowing dimly in the darkness.

He rubbed his eyes and walked away into the kitchen wondering if maybe this time the caller might be genuine.

Ridiculous.

Alex pushed the idea out of his head and walked to the fridge.

Inside felt as warm as the outside since the power hadn't returned.

Still, warm Sprite was better than no Sprite.

He took the bottle and unscrewed the top. Now he could hear the gentle fizzing of his drink that sounded almost soothing, if not for the phone.

Disconnect it, he told himself.

He wasn't so stupid he hadn't thought of that, of course he had, but something stopped him. What if he disconnected it and it continued to ring. Now he was being childish. Too many late night horror movies on channel five.

What if you disconnect it and you never hear your mother's voice again?

Fuck you, he told himself.

Just go next door and pull that nicotine stained chord out of its socket to disconnect it.

He took another sip of sprite and paced the kitchen floor. The place was a mess with boxes he still hadn't unpacked since he moved in last week. On one box he could see the thick marker pen writing which read 'ANGELA'S STUFF'

His mind, lost in the darkness of the room almost blotted out the phone ringing when Angela, the ex from hell, came to mind. He could almost picture her lying in bed with…suddenly the ringer sounded like it was mocking him and he wondered if somehow it could be the ex from hell ringing up, playing a sick joke with whatever guy she was with now.

He really needed to post the box of her belongings, or throw it away. He doubted she'd miss a few Madonna albums and books she'd read.

Suddenly he was walking through to the hallway and towards the ringing phone which was now starting to sound like it was screaming at him.

Quickly and without hesitation, he walked towards the phone.

As he got closer and squatted down over it, he became overpowered with a sudden smell which made him drop the half bottle of Sprite and tip back onto one hand.

'It can't be,' he whispered as he leant closer to the phone.

'There's no way,' he said moving his head closer.

He took a short scared breath in through his nose but there was nothing. He tried again, this time taking in a bigger breath, but still nothing.

Yet for a second he was sure, he had smelt his mother's perfume. He didn't question it because he was certain. He'd recognise the cheap, eye-stinging scent anywhere. It used to engulf the house when she was getting ready to go out with his father. Quickly he got to his feet and walked away backwards from the phone and although he couldn't smell that cheap potent smell, it was lodged in his head, opening up hundreds of memories he'd forgotten all about.

His eyes suddenly began to feel very heavy.

Alex sat on the sofa in the living room wishing he had a torch or some candles.

Lost, remembering his life from long ago, from when he was happiest, when his mother hadn't been raped by that disease, a time when she still had a few more summers of youthfulness on her side. Closing his eyes, he let the memories flood him...

*

He must have been six or seven when they were a whole family. They were at the beach in Alnmouth.

His father was wearing a white open shirt and denim jeans. His mother wore a long floral dress. Her hair was long then and he could see it clearly, all golden and shining in the sea air. They were having a picnic on the sand. It could have been a postcard photo, it felt that perfect.

Out at sea Alex watched a ship. It wasn't moving. Close to the rocks, the sunlight bounced on the water, making Alex think someone had dropped pieces of glass on the surface.

He'd forgotten just how good-looking his parents had been. Perhaps that was why his dad had strayed to the woman he employed to be his personal assistant, a woman Alex had heard his mother refer to as "that slut". But that would come later, years later. Right now they were a family, they were happy and enjoying a summer at the beach.

So why did his mother look so lost.

The young Alex can smell the egg sandwiches his mother has made. He knows they'll get bits of sand in them no matter how hard he tries.

They always did.

He looks at his mother as she hands him one. She smiles but he can see something is on her mind. He couldn't see it back then, but now in memory it's plain to see.

He turns and his father is gazing out towards the ocean liner. He looks lost too. Alex turned back to his mother and realises she knows, even before he told her, even right here in a day Alex always thought was perfect, she knows his father has been having an affair.

Alex sprung awake to the darkness of his flat.

His head was swimming and he could hear his mother whispering in a deep corner of his mind that it was the salt air making him tired.

Gently he closed his eyes, just to rest them again, not to sleep, not to…

*

The room was white. The whitest he'd ever seen a

room. So white it almost glowed and stunk of disinfectant. There was one window, which looked out towards a lake where ducks circled. He wasn't sure of the time, wasn't sure of anything any more. On the surface of the lake there were speckles of sunlight, reflecting and bouncing like shards of glass. It felt late, a late summer night. He walked closer to the window and that was when he saw the bed sticking out from behind the door. It too was white.

Alex turned and saw a skeleton-like body in the bed. An old and dying woman that sent shivers up his body. No, it was worse than that. This felt like, if he had a soul, it too was shivering.

He walked closer to the bed and his mind told him to stop being stupid. To stop fooling himself into pretending this woman was a stranger.

It was his mother.

Alex swallowed and his throat made a clicking sound.

It can't be, he thought.

He gazed down at the woman. She looked about one hundred, but he knew she was only sixty-six. Her hair, what was left of it, hung over her shoulders colourlessly.

Her cheekbones looked like they were trying to poke through her yellow cracked skin and her mouth was covered in thick saliva.

Alex didn't know he was crying, crying so hard, but not looking away from the woman he'd thought always looked so radiant, the woman who once turned heads everywhere she went.

He wanted to say something, but when he opened his mouth nothing come out. He looked into her eyes and there was nothing; those large blue globes he had also inherited were lost and unfocussed. She couldn't see him or she was blind, and then at that moment as he opened his mouth, he heard the clicking of shoes and gasped when he saw his aunt Ruth enter the room.

She moved around him towards the bed. No that was wrong. She moved through him towards the bed.

'Hey Pamela how's it going?' said Aunt Ruth.

Alex glanced down and saw his mother's eyes flicker slightly and her mouth twist almost painfully into a smile.

'Did you reach him?' said his mother tiredly.

Alex felt his eyes drowning with tears again. This was what happened when she died, he told himself.

It had been a long time ago when the end

had come and he had forgotten most of it, mostly because he hadn't been there. He had been living in France with Angela and although his mother had been ill and coping for years, when he received the phone call and left France that night, she was dead by the time he got to the hospital in London. Sometimes he thought he knew the exact moment she died too, like he'd felt it when he had been on the plane. And now he was in the room with her, only she couldn't see him.

'We phoned Alex and he's on his way back,' said Aunt Ruth.

'He doesn't have to…'said his Pamela, her voice fading off.

'He wants too' said Ruth as she tucked in the covers around her youngest sister.

'We argued when we last spoke…'

'That doesn't matter now' said Ruth, her voice showing signs of strain.

He remembered the argument. When he told her he was leaving for France and she'd shouted to him that it wouldn't last with Angela. Really she was just scared for him. He knew that, of course he knew that, because hindsight was a beautiful thing. But at the time, he shouted back, even when she was in her home, too ill to make herself a cup of tea; he'd shouted back something about needing to live his own life. Then he'd walked out slamming the door to his mother's faint cry. In that moment he was sure he'd told her to leave him alone.

Why was I such dick, he thought, why was I such a poor excuse of a son?

He'd phoned her from the airport before leaving and made a promise to come back the next week when he got things settled in France but like all good sons, he never did, thinking there'd always be time.

A few months later she was gone.

Back in the room Alex had stepped away from the bed, but couldn't take his eyes off his mother.

'I want to tell Alex...' she said.

'Just relax Pam, you will...'

His mother twisted angrily and then her eyes...

She could see him, he was certain she was looking right at him. A smile gently crept upon her face, bringing a faint reflection of the woman she had been.

Alex looked back and opened his mouth, but before anything was said, there was a flash. Like all the whiteness of the room had exploded and when Alex opened his eyes he was back in the darkness of his own flat, in his own time.

His eyes were wet from tears. He knew now, that everything he had done since her death had been filled with guilt and remorse.

Angela had told him he'd been crazy to think his mother resented him or was disappointed in him, but it always lingered on his mind and had effect on everything. He supposed that was what drove Angela away, his own self loathing.

The phone continued to ring.

Suddenly, with the urgency of a slap across the face, Alex was on his feet. His eyes were streaming with tears and he could feel his chest heaving. He ran into the hallway and towards the phone which didn't look like it was glowing anymore, now it really was glowing, the brightest cleanest hospital white he had ever seen.

He grabbed the receiver and picked it up.

'Alex?' a voice he recognised right away.

'Mum, its Alex' his voice almost a whisper.

There was a pause and then 'I want you to know Alex that I don't forgive you,' his mother said.

Alex felt his eyes burning with tears as he tried to keep it together.

'I don't forgive you for leaving me Alex.'

There was another pause and Alex forced himself to grip the phone with both hands.

'I don't forgive you because I never blamed you for going to France' she said, sounding almost youthful again.

'You don't?' was all he could say as the tears began to choke him.

'Of course I don't. I love you, son. I never said how proud I am of you son so I'm saying it now. I am proud of you and I'm so sorry things didn't work out with Angela.'

'Mum, where are you?'

'There's no time for that' she said quickly. 'Just know that I'm safe and happy and son...?'

'Will I see you again?' he asked, almost hating his voice for how broken it was sounding.

'Of course you will,' she said followed by a short laugh, 'and things are going to get better for you,' she continued. 'You might not see it now, but trust me, I know things are going to get better.'

He opened his mouth, wanting to say he loved her. In all his life he couldn't remember saying it, but as his lips parted, he found himself speechless.

'Listen Alex I don't have much time. If

they knew I was communicating this way I would get into a lot of trouble.'

'I'm sorry for what…when we argued,' said Alex.

'I know you are son, I knew you never meant it.'

Alex was sobbing now and not gently. He steadied himself against the wall.

'I have to go now Alex. You take care my darling. I love you.'

'I love you,' he gasped. 'I love you.'

And before there was a reply, the line was dead.

Alex dropped the phone to the floor and sat down crying in the dark and wondered if he would ever stop crying. He had a lot of tears to make up for.

Alone and in the darkness he felt a weight lifting from him, deep within.

*

When Alex lifted his head from the floor morning light was creeping into the windows. He sat up and felt like his back was broken. He hadn't forgotten the phone call and it hadn't seemed like a dream.

In fact, he picked up the receiver just to see if his mother was on the line, but there was nothing.

He got up and tried the hallway light, discovering at long last that the power had been restored.

He walked into the kitchen smiling, turning on the light as he entered.

Things were going to get better; he felt it in his heart. Something he had been carrying with him for a long time had gone.

Now things would get better.

He turned and looked back at the mysterious phone, and wondered if he'd ever have another phone call from his mother.

He doubted it.

Yet in many ways it didn't matter. She would never be far away.

SURVIVORS

They were the last two survivors. That was what Chris Dean was starting to believe. He had been travelling with James Briggs for the past month.

At first, during the early days, neither had bothered to speak unless it was necessary. In that time Chris had tortured himself thinking who Briggs, with his big frame and black, thinning, out of control hair, looked like. There was something in the eyes. After the third day, it came to Chris and he burst out laughing. When James asked what was so funny Chris just shook his head.

James Briggs was a dead ringer for old school magician/comedian Tommy Cooper. In every physical detail, down to the way he spoke and on the odd occasion, the way he smiled, but that was where it ended.

Briggs was neither funny nor comical.

He was a lost man, lost in his own thoughts, lost in the past and at night, lost in his dreams.

Sometimes Chris would listen as Briggs dreamed. In his sleep Briggs would laugh a haunting crazed laugh that was filled with so much pain it almost sounded like crying. There were other nights too when he kept telling someone he was sorry, someone he called Katie.

That was where the emotional side of Briggs ended, in dreams. During the days of their journey, the big man stayed strong not even batting an eye when they found the body of a young girl hanging from a tree branch, her insides on the outside glistening like rubies.

They still had not crossed any of the enemy yet but then they never stopped to look for them since the Grems had a way of creeping up and had crept up on so many people since their arrival on the planet that now the population was dominated by the sluggish creatures.

But here they were - the two survivors, within the last ten miles of a hundred-mile journey; almost within sight of the alleged safety zone, a place where secure units had been set up by other survivors; a place which was supposedly impossible for the Grems to invade.

Chris had only seen one of the aliens close up and it reminded him of Jabba the Hutt from Return of the Jedi. But, he'd been told these sluggish creatures weren't slow, they could move fast.

Chris had watched one die. Its blackened eyes looking up at him, its huge mouth hanging open in an O shape and drooling a thick brown liquid that smelt of vinegar. Chris had wanted to shoot it. To put the foul beast out of its misery but instead he just watched, as it rolled its yellow body from side to side dying in torment.

Both men sat down on the grassy embankment sipping water from their canteens. Chris's legs ached and he kept expecting Briggs to tell him it was time to keep moving, but he did not. It seemed the big man was just as exhausted.

Chris glanced over the grassy embankment towards the horizon and hoped what he would find on the other side would be the safety zone, looking the way it had looked in his dreams.

A cold shiver suddenly jittered down his back.

He hoped they'd have a cold glass of beer waiting for him, with beads of condensation running down the glass.

That was enough reason to not give up; even though he was sure his big toe was broken.

They both wore black clothes to stay camouflaged at night. Briggs wore a long wool coat that stank of B/O, but Chris was used to the smell now and it sure looked warmer than Chris's leather jacket.

There had only been one other time in his life when he had felt the kind of fear he was feeling now. The first time had been ten years ago when he was fourteen and came home from school to find his two rabbits, Starsky and Hutch, dead, their heads hanging on by a few loose, red chords and Patsy, the stray neighbourhood dog, standing nearby, her mouth caked in dry blood and clumps of white hairs. This shock was different but still shared the same, stomach bubbling intensity. He was scared, afraid that when they crossed the horizon there would be nothing.

No safety zone.

What if the reports and signals they had heard were wrong. What if over the next hill there were armies of Grems all waiting to pounce.

He'd heard it was a painful process being eaten by a Grem. Their long slug like bodies could cocoon a man in seconds and then pulsate, sucking at him like a boiled sweet until there was nothing left but bone and teeth.

Chris shivered.

Briggs had told him stories of his battles with the Grems, explaining that he had killed one and found three almost decomposed bodies inside. Chris hated the way Briggs was so animated and enthusiastic when he talked about death.

They sat there for over an hour in silence. Chris thinking about his sister Lana, wondering if she had gotten out of the city before the major invasion, hoping against hope that she was in the safety zone.

'What's on your mind lad?' asked Briggs loudly as he cleaned his rifle.

'I'm scared,' Chris said. 'I'm scared of what we'll find when we cross that hill.'

James looked upwards and outwards to the horizon. 'Either way we'll find out soon.'

Chris saw fear in Briggs's eyes; fear he knew the big man couldn't hide forever.

'Do you have any family?' asked Chris.

Briggs stared at his feet. Chris had an idea that his companion's memories were slowly catching up with him.

It took a while and when there was no reply, Chris said,

'I guess we should keep moving, it'll be too hard to spot the Grems at night.'

Briggs swallowed and his throat made a dry clicking sound.

'There was someone once,' he said 'She was called Katie.'

'What happened?' asked Chris.

The big man shook his head and smiled a

wide joker-like grin, making an image of Tommy Cooper pop into Chris's head, a sight he quickly discarded.

> 'I would like to think she is still alive somewhere' said James before laughing wildly. 'I would like to think she is over that hill.' He shouted hysterically before bursting into tears.

Chris grabbed the big man before he could think and held his head against his chest listening to his friend cry and talk at the same time, none of his words making any real sense.

By the time nightfall came Chris and Briggs were ready to walk the remaining ten miles. As they sorted out their supplies, Chris heard a ticking sound from behind him.

The sound of a Grem.

'We left it too long,' Chris shouted, swinging his rifle from his shoulder.

When he turned Briggs was already stood behind him, rifle in hands looking west.

'That was one of them right?' asked Chris. 'You think they followed us?'

James lowered his gun and turned to Chris.

'We should go now,' he said, in a whisper Chris did not think the big man was capable of.

Suddenly Chris felt a deep gag in his throat caused by…

It was the foul Grem odour.

They were close.

Holding his rifle in one hand he quickly put his shirt over his mouth.

'They must be close, damn it!' he shouted.

Briggs looked over the horizon his face was sweating scared.

'Do you see anything?' shouted Chris as he ran to where his friend stood.

Quickly he stopped.

On the horizon, in the moonlight there were shapes, moving and pulsating shapes that made Chris raise his rifle and start shooting.

Suddenly the big man's strong hand grabbed the gun from Chris and threw it to the ground.

'What are you doing?' barked Chris, his whole body shaking.

James walked a few steps and turned around. Chris could see his face clearly in the moonlight. All similarities to the old comedian Tommy Cooper were gone. Now there was nothing.

'It's often wondered how the Grem can catch a victim with its slow moving body and defenceless shape. People still have not figured out how the Grems killed everyone in London last year. People never took the time. They tried to kill us when they should have studied us a little better, in the same way we spent decades studying you. All we wanted was peace.'

'What are you talking about… Us?' demanded Chris.

'I am talking about our greatest weapon, disguise.'

Chris slowly bent his knees eyeing his rifle below his feet.

'I liked you Chris, I enjoyed studying your habits and ways. It will not go to waste I promise you that, and thanks for leading us to the safe zone.'

'But your wife, Katie!'

James smiled and pondered everything for a moment and then explained how he'd made her up after studying someone else. That she was all just part of a story.

Suddenly there was a ripping sound followed by an awful cracking which turned into a succession of ticks.

Chris froze, not comprehending what he

was seeing.

James Briggs was gone. Where he once stood was a large Grem, its glistening body covered in hundreds of thick sharp black hairs. On the floor below it was its human costume.

Slowly it pulsated, moving towards Chris in a succession of squelching and deflating sounds.

Chris turned away quickly, ready to run.

As he did so, he was greeted by four more large Grems.

After that they were on him.

After that there was nothing.

THE SALESMAN

It was a hot July. Prickly heat was making the Salesman want to scream and several times he did. The passer-by didn't hear him as he yelled at him over his car stereo. The old hag at the zebra crossing didn't respond when he screamed at her to get a fucking move on. It seemed no one in the town was interested in what the Salesman had to offer.

All the road signs told him he was in Yardale, but he could have sworn it was Wesburn. He was certain that a year ago when he came to this shit-tip that the name of the town was different. Everything but the relentless heat seemed to have changed.

Fifty-six and still selling insurance to morons. This wasn't the life David Sullivan had wanted. It wasn't bad, it had its perks but fuck, he was fed up of playing the nice guy, preaching and practically begging the idiot nation to sign its life away.

He had hoped to retire at fifty. What a joke that had been. Still, the idea hadn't changed. Retire, move to Switzerland or some country where he'd never wake up hot again in his life. Screw cheap women, whose best years were behind them. Maybe even keep his wife on, instead of pissing all his earnings away in a divorce.

Angela wasn't a bad wife he supposed. Nothing to look at. Piss poor in bed. Yet she was loyal and kept the house in a good condition. Jenny, her brat, his slob step-daughter, was another story. She was lazy, jobless and thought the world owed her a living. She still lived at home, too. Age twenty-two and still leeching off her mother. He couldn't pretend she was his. He'd met Angela when Jenny was sixteen and he hated her. Neither love nor respect came with time for either party.

Some nights he'd listen to her fucking her lesbian girlfriends, as Angela would pretend it wasn't happening. He didn't understand lesbians. Jenny had no choice; a man wouldn't look twice at her flabby arse, but some of the girls she brought home… It was a mystery why they chose a fat opinionated bitch like Jenny. Some of them weren't half bad by any standards. One he remembered Jenny had been seeing for a few months. She'd had brilliantly tits. Wasted on Jenny, he thought. Still, he enjoyed hearing her moan through the ceiling. One thing about Jenny, she seemed more versed in fucking than Angela did.

He parked the car at the side of the road, doubtful if he'd get a ticket. Fuck them anyway he thought. *Let the company pay for it if I get fined.*

He got out the car and glanced up the street to the cluster of shops. There was no one on main street. The once-busy town he remembered was empty. Still, he thought, wiping his top lip, there must be someone I can sell insurance too.

Where was the old hag that had crossed the road?

Didn't I pass some kids way back?

He looked across to where more shops were situated but couldn't see her or anyone else. A red neon sign said OPEN in the front of the newsagents and the Salesman pondered the idea of buying a few cold Cokes but then decided against it.

Damn, it's hot! he said to no-one, as he began wiping a line of sweat from his brow. It was always too hot. Too hot to work and even too hot to smoke, but he smoked anyway as he formulated a plan. Have a drink, his mind told him, *one for the job as you decide which street to hit.* Find a row of bungalows with the aged in them. He could get them to sign up for anything as long as he promised them a free clock and used his presidential trustworthy smile.

He pressed the alarm on his car keys and waited for it to make its double beep sound.

There was a pub over the road called 'New Beginnings'. A pretentious, hipster-looking bar he thought, *but wasn't it called the Three Lions or something last time?*

Places change but lager doesn't and that's what he needed; that and a nice air- conditioned corner to rest his sopping balls that felt like they had been lost in a swamp between his legs.

He crossed the empty road and walked towards the bar with the sun on his back, slowly frying his large, already red, roll of a neck.

A few empty chairs and tables were outside the pub.

Where is everybody? he wondered when suddenly the door to the pub burst open and someone ran out, almost knocking him off his feet.

The Salesman shouted but the hooded stranger paid no notice and blitzed up the street. *What the hell is that kid holding?* thought the Salesman.

Is that a fake leg?

It sure looked that way as the shadowy figure ran up the middle of the deserted road.

'Fucking kids,' he muttered.

Then he noticed the BMW parked outside the bar. There were a few other cars parked along the street, but this one had its front passenger door wide open.

Couldn't leave your car like that in my street, he thought as he walked closer.

He peered in and saw an A-Z on the front seat. Least he wasn't the only person that still used them. He hated sat-nav. It always got him lost; always lost signal. Things that were supposed to make the world work faster always fucked up or needed charging.

He stepped back to the bar, pushed open the door and walked inside the pub.

There was something at the bar. It made him stop suddenly and forget about the heat. His legs started shaking slightly, like a dumb cartoon character.

He didn't know what it...

An animal or...

It looked back at him, slurping its drink through a straw. Its eyes were completely black and dead. Purple veins streaked up its long grey face, like road maps, to the creature's temples. A small mouth closed around the straw. Its body was slouched and grey. Ribs and bones stuck through its skin making it look malnourished.

On the floor was a mess of blood and chunks of body. They were in a heap and the Salesman gasped when he saw the pulse beat several times, like they were still alive.

The Salesman quickly spun on the spot and grabbed the door to leave.

The door was locked.

He tried it again.

Still locked.

'How long have you been standing there?' asked the thing at the bar and when the Salesman turned back he saw a woman staring back at him.

He wondered if it had been the heat fucking with him. As a kid, he'd had sunstroke once and thought he heard his dead brother shouting his name to come and get dinner.

His head was beating with a fantastic migraine that had suddenly erupted without warning. He wiped his eyes which were stinging dry like burning pinballs and looked at the bar, trying to do anything to get what he'd thought he'd seen from his head.

What I saw, he wondered.

Something bad.

He was sure it was...

A young woman with flowing blonde hair smiled back at him and the Salesman's mouth lifted into a cracked smile.

I could have a good time with that, he thought.

She looked early-twenties.

He wondered what it was about that stare. It was like she was undressing him with her eyes. She was trying to imagine what was behind his shirt and trousers, which was crazy. No-one would ever look at him like that. He might be horny but he wasn't stupid. At fifty-six any good looks he might have held in his late teens had gone, hidden behind a beer belly, a mask of wrinkled skin and a balding nest of hair.

Yet, it didn't stop the punishing lust he had for her. He looked down at the floor and the remains he'd imagined had gone, leaving no stains on the carpet.

'I said how long were you standing there?'

The Salesman gasped.

'It isn't a hard question, is it?' she said.

'Not long,' he said gingerly.

He wanted to say something about what he saw but his head throbbed repeatedly.

The woman slowly took a sip from her glass, not bothering with the straw. He was sure she knew he wanted to fuck her. Right here, right now, on the bar if she liked. It didn't matter to him. He'd done it in stranger places. The hunger he felt for her was foreign to him. Sure he'd had burning desires before, but this was almost overpowering, to the point it was hurting just to look at her.

Her tan looked real. No orange or marks where it had faded or been washed off. Her skin was perfectly browned and he was sure it would taste as good as it looked.

She had a kind and warm face and when she smiled at him it was an infectious grin he couldn't help return.

'I said, tell me what you saw when you walked in here.'

The Salesman had almost forgotten what he'd seen, was almost convinced now it had all been sunstroke. All he was sure was what he was seeing now. A young woman, no older than his bitchy, fat step-daughter.

'I only just walked in when you turned around.'

'Now why don't I believe you?' she said provocatively.

A cold draft blew over his body.

Perhaps she was right. There was something else to remember.

Something about the way she looked at him was making him forget everything, like it was just pouring out of his head, including the migraine.

Go to her.

The Salesman slowly moved across to the bar and sat down facing her. Those eyes are as blue as the ocean he thought, romantically.

She was drinking a glass of lemonade. Although it could have been gin and tonic, the idea of tasting her lips and mouth, sweetened with lemonade, made him smile. It looked cold and the beads of icy sweat running down the glass made him thirsty.

'You want some?' she said and pushed him the glass.

'Thanks,' he replied before taking a long drink from the glass.

It wasn't lemonade. It wasn't gin either. He wasn't sure what it was but it tasted good and sweet.

He looked down and saw her tanned cleavage and then his eyes shifted to her crossed legs. There were secrets to be had in between those legs he was sure.

'Do you like what you see?' she asked turning on her chair towards him.

He couldn't stop staring at her breasts.

Even if he tried he couldn't. Shit this wasn't like him. Yes, he was sexist and would take any pussy on offer but he liked to think he had some reserve and some control, yet here he was behaving like a dog on heat.

The Salesman tried and managed to look up into her tender inviting, eyes.

'Do you want to touch me then?' she asked pushing a strand of her blonde hair behind her ear.

His hands shook. Before he could reach out she was pulling down her dress revealing her firm, hand sized breasts. The nipples and areolas were pink and desperately hurting him to look at. He let out a tiny gasp of pure amazement.

He wanted to touch her, grab those tits and…but there was that warning sign again, echoing way off in his mind, it tried to tell him something was amiss.

Why is a young, fit woman offering it to a fat sweaty prick like you, so easily?

He didn't care.

He didn't even care if it was a set up. If Angela and his bitch step-daughter had paid some whore to catch him out. *She maybe wants a divorce and*…fuck it he didn't care because all that mattered was…

Suddenly his headache was gone, along with any control he might have had.

He pressed his hand on her leg and it felt soft and warmed by the heat.

His breathing suddenly began to speed up. A million scenarios rushed through his head, and all involved the two of them naked on the bar.

Her smell was intoxicatingly brilliant. He'd never smelt a woman or perfume as good. He wanted to smother his head in her breasts forever and take in a deep breath when suddenly...

Grey.

Suddenly the leg had turned grey and wet beneath his hand. His imagination had ended. He felt the headache return but with it his common sense came too. He looked at his hand which was touching a watery, grey leg that felt like jellied eels.

Grey.

Everywhere, she was grey.

He looked up and saw the creature staring back at him perversely from its black, lifeless, shark-like eyes.

It sat dome-shaped on the seat, like some sort of prehistoric sea creature. A cross between a seal and some sort of twisted old mutated alien from those dumb conspiracy, Area 51, videos.

The thing's mouth hung open, revealing tiny razor-sharp yellowed teeth. Halitosis was ripe with the foul creature and the Salesman gasped. The thing turned its head and looked at him indifferently, before letting out a moan that sounded pure agony.

Quickly he turned to jump from his chair and run when, instantly, the creature was on him, sucking and ripping at his body.

He fell backwards off the chair and it followed him, only now there were others, all viciously fighting over what the Salesman had to offer.

They all looked the same, although some were shorter and others tall. There was no waiting turns though. The bigger ones pushed the smaller ones aside and got stuck in.

There's enough to go around ladies – but these things weren't ladies. One of them was running out of the door holding something of his – *a leg* he thought.

He looked down and saw they had somehow torn it away from the knee down. *Strange I can still feel my foot.*

He glanced to the side where a small creature held his hand, tenderly tearing his nails off one by one and then chewing them like crisps. Blood poured from his fingers and another creature was quick to lick it away, like a melting ice-cream.

The creature that started it all was lying by his side spooning his body. Gently, it started kissing his neck, licking away sweat with a bloated and blackened tongue.

When it reached his mouth, it's tongue wrapped itself around his tongue and tore it free – but there was no pain.

He saw his stomach open and a host of slime-covered, glistening fingers taking out his major organs – still though, no pain.

They tossed the intestines between each other. Biting them open and squeezing out the juices. Another tucked into the stomach, tearing it open and marvelling at what it had to offer.

Dome heads stared down at him, sweating grey droplets onto his face as they enjoyed his offerings.

The darkness came soon – one of them, he didn't know which, had sucked out his eyes and he could hear them being swallowed in loud gulps.

His penis was still hard but he wasn't sure if they had taken that also as clusters of fingers ripped and pulled at his balls.

After what felt like minutes, he felt his head drifting, and he was certain the bar had been called the Three Lions last time he was in it, and he was sure these creatures had dined on everyone in the piss ant of a town.

Suddenly fingers were poking in through his eye sockets. Scrapping towards his brain.

Still there was no pain, just a weird feeling of his mind and body departing from one another.

He thought for a quick second of Angela and his bitch stepdaughter and then there was nothing.

The creatures pulled the meat from the bones, eating silently and quickly. It didn't take long before the entire Salesman's major workings were gone. Smaller creatures now picked at bones and stuffed clusters of skin into their mouths, savouring each morsel.

Fat poured from the body but even this had its uses at the larger creatures scooped it up and rubbed it into their skin for reasons known only to them.

The creature the Salesman had desperately wanted to get inside of had retired back to her chair holding a pulpy mess of brain. She ate it slowly watching the other creatures as they wandered back out of the room to where they had been waiting.

Once the brain was gone the creature

burped a long, wretched noise and thought, I've eaten too much.

THE PRIEST AND THE WITCH

The priest was a drunk, they all knew that and that was why they stayed away from the church.

The pews were empty, just as they had been empty for the previous five Sundays. He told himself it was the people's fault, that they had stopped believing. He told himself they had lost faith.

But recently he had accepted the truth. A cold truth he had always known; the people had lost faith in him.

He had tried but had forgotten when the drinking had spiralled out of control. There had been no great tragedy in his forty-nine years. All his life the only person he had ever really been close to was God and He had never abandoned him. Yet still sometimes, Father Jeffery Lawson wondered if anyone above was listening to him. He looked down the centre aisle and remembered all the weddings and funerals he'd participated in over the years, all the tender moments of both rejoicing and mourning.

Where did all the years go?
The quiet charm of the morning always moved him.

Gently he stepped down from behind the altar and walked to the first row of seats. Blue bibles were scattered along them with afternoon sunlight shining on their hard covers.

Timeless sunlight he thought; in God's house time stood still.

The silence was beautiful.
It felt like the world had stopped.

He never got tired of the stillness of time within his church. This building had been here for hundreds of years, and thousands of people had passed through it. Sometimes when he closed his eyes he could almost hear them, the long-forgotten voices of days gone.

He picked up one of the tattered bibles and smelt the spine. He loved that smell. But this time it made him crave a drink. Anything beautiful or mournful went better with single malt.

Where did it all go wrong he wondered, placing the book back down on the seat?

His body was thin now, since the drinking had surpassed any need he had for food. His face was tired and red, bloated in places and an alarming shade of purple creased around his yellowing eyes.

He walked down the aisle to the main doors. By the entrance, he glanced at the donations box but had given up checking it.

It was always empty.

He opened the great door and stepped out. The air smelled great. He often wished he'd been placed in a church with gardens or a cemetery, but High Fell church had neither. All there was to see was a lonely road, which ran up a steep hill towards the town. There was a council cemetery and crematorium on the opposite side of the road though, a place Father Lawson had liked to go to in the early days when he wanted to reflect. From where he stood, he could smell the Oak trees and they still smelt wonderful. He hoped when he died he was buried under one of them.

He glanced at his watch, and saw that three in the afternoon was an acceptable time for a trip to town to do some shopping and...

He was fooling himself.

He would go to town and drink. Perhaps have a conversation with a few of the other town locals.

Why keep pretending, he thought.
He turned from the main doors and when he did, he forgot the ideas of drunken opinions and glasses of whiskey. In front of him, standing behind the last pew was a boy, no older than eight. Jeffrey didn't recognise the boy as he walked closer, but these days he had difficulty remembering most people.

'Are you the priest?' asked the boy politely.

An odd question, thought Jeffrey, considering what he was wearing.

'Yes lad, I am. What can I do for you?' asked Jeffrey as he approached the boy.

'You have to come quick,' said the boy. 'There is a witch in the cemetery. I saw her.'

The priest didn't laugh.

He wondered how many of the kid's friends were hiding outside. A good old-fashioned dare. But before Jeffrey could ask, the boy started crying. Not gently or quietly. The boy was crying in great heavy wails.

Letting go of something that had been troubling him for so long, thought Jeffrey. He could relate to that.

Jeffery walked closer and placed a hand on the boy's shoulder.

'Son?' he asked softly.

The boy wiped away his tears but couldn't say the words until his chest had stop up heaving.

'I can take you there. It's not far, just around the corner' said the boy, his eyes focussed and intense.

'I know where the cemetery is lad.'

The boy nodded.

Jeffrey stepped back. He wondered if perhaps the boy was being abused at home. The kid looked undernourished and his white shirt was torn slightly around the collar and blackened with dirt. Also, the child's trousers were faded from black to grey and he smelt like he hadn't bathed in months.

'First tell me your name' asked Jeffrey 'and then tell me who has been hurting you.'

'My name is Karl,' said the boy softly, 'and the witch hurt me.'

Perhaps he's using the word witch when he means his mother, or aunt or grandmother.

Jeffrey walked around the pews and sat down next to the boy, nodding for the boy to sit down too.

The boy sat down and wiped his face.

'I didn't know where else to go. No one believes me,' said the boy, bursting into more tears.

'What about your parents, have you told them?' asked Jeffrey.

'There's not enough time. She's very angry. Only you can stop her.'

He supposed it wouldn't take long to put the boy's mind at rest. He'd take his mobile though. Just in case there was a nut job in the cemetery. He could walk from there afterwards for a drink, and that idea made everything have more of a purpose.

'Come on then son, let's go and see this witch,' said the priest standing up.

'Will you, I mean can you get rid of the witch?' said the boy in a frail, hopeless voice.

Jeffrey smiled, 'Of course I can, don't you know about Salem?'

'What is Salem?' asked the boy confused.

'Never mind. Come on, let's go and find this witch.'

The boy's face lit up into a smile. He leapt forward and embraced Jeffrey. It was good to be held again, thought Jeffrey. Good to be needed.

They both stood up and the priest held the kid's hand as they walked back towards the entrance.

'Don't you need holy water and bible?' asked the boy.

The Priest not wanting to upset the child, told him he had them under his smock as he opened the large church doors.

Of course, he was lying.

*

The graveyard was full of people. The priest wondered at first if perhaps there was a funeral taking place.

Then he felt bitter that it wasn't a service he was part of.

He looked down at the boy who clung to his hand.

To his left several children stood together. They watched him eagerly as he walked along the main road further into the cemetery.

To his left a large cluster of people stood talking, all without concern for the priest and the boy.

Jeffrey tried to pay no attention to them.

'She's by that building' said the boy pointing towards the crematorium.

The priest continued and saw a young girl, no older than seventeen sitting in the road by the building. She had long, flowing ribbons of blonde hair which swirled around her face in the wind. He could hear her cries long before he reached her. When she looked up at him her cheeks were flushed with pink and soaked with tears.

When she saw Father Lawson she stared at him for a long time, her eyes red from crying.

'I'm sorry. I didn't mean to bring them back, I was angry,' she said softly.

'Bring who back?' said the priest calmly.

'I was angry. Please, I was looking for my father but he's not here.'

'Who came back?' he asked gently.

'All of them,' she said and pointed to the crematorium.

The priest walked away from the girl, with the boy still clinging to his hand. He went around the opposite east side of the crematorium, where the pathway turned in an oval shape, and when the girl was out of sight the priest let go of the boy's hand.

At the north side of the graveyard he saw them and stopped.

Hundreds of people, none of them moving, some in groups and some standing alone.

All their eyes on him. All their faces blackened from dirt.

He looked across from them to the graves and saw every plot of land was open. Mounds of earth were stacked by each grave, some with caskets lying open next to them. It was like someone had dug up every grave in the place or...

Suddenly everything felt like slow motion. The priest felt his legs shivering and as he fell to the floor, he saw the boy watching him in fear.

He landed on his behind, which caused a sharp pain in his coccyx.

'She brought us all back,' said the boy, 'and we didn't want to come back. It hurts, it hurts so much to be here,' moaned the boy.

He looked up and into the boy's eyes. They were devoid of colour and life.

How didn't I see it before?

Quickly he got back to his feet. The boy moved closer to him and when he held out a hand the priest shoved him to the ground.

Shadows suddenly covered the boy. The priest looked up and saw the dead were moving towards him.

All their faces pleading, wanting redemption, crying for salvation with the boy leading them.

Quickly he ran back around the crematorium.

The girl was gone.

'I told you she was a witch!' shouted the boy following him.

How had I not noticed the funeral attire they all wore?

The filthy clothes from their burial ground.

'She brought us back, Mr' said the boy, 'and some of us are very angry.'

The priest gazed down at the boy's face. His eyes were sunken. His lips blue. *How hadn't I known the kid was dead.*

Suddenly a young toddler dressed in a silk ivory suit was tugging at his trousers. The priest pushed himself away and the toddler fell to the floor crying a haunting, crackled moan.

He quickly turned to run and felt the kid's hand dragging him.

'Help us....' someone shouted.

'Save us!' another cried.

The priest turned and saw the dead were

inches from him, all crying out for something.
    He closed his eyes.
    Tried to wish them all away but it was too late.
    In the end, he was needed after all.

WICKED WAYS

It seemed like a dream, a dream of a time and place he had visited before in his sleep. It began as it always had with him…

*

…sitting on a gently sloping rise that overlooks the athletic fields at his old high-school. The rise is the highest point in town and for miles in any direction in the otherwise flat landscape of the Mississippi Delta. It is a blazing hot day in early-May, the sky a cloudless cobalt dome. The windshields of nearby parked cars shine like diamonds in the sun; there is a pleasant smell of freshly cut grass in the breeze that tickles his nose. Sitting with him is his father, whose unruly mop of red hair flips about his face in the breeze. His gold rimmed glasses stick up on his head, all but lost in the nest of hair. He is wearing one of his white shirts and dark ties. David Moore always wore a tie when he worked at Kirby Home Video, back when videos and renting them was new and exciting.

But there is so much about this little scene that just seems all wrong. Why is he trapped in such a timeless and eerie feeling? A feeling that has so warped his senses that he feels like the man of thirty-eight he is, a man with tattoos on both arms, instead of the seven-year-old kid he has always been before in the dream.

If a dream is what this truly is. He isn't

sure...can't seem to figure it out.

Equally troubling is why the hell is he feeling so weirdly nostalgic to be sitting there with his father—his dead father, the man years in his grave—and thinking, as if trying to convince himself, how good things were when he was a kid of seven? He has never dreamed that things were good when he was that age because they were anything but that. By then both his father and mother had started drinking, and that was because his sister, Lanie, had...

...had what? Something had happened to her, but he can't seem to remember what. He is puzzled and angered by that, and yet it isn't the most disturbing thing about this.

How the hell can he be dreaming when he knows damn good and well he isn't asleep?

Yet the dream, or whatever this may be, is beginning to feel more and more like the nightmare it has always been. The bright light of strength and wisdom he first noticed in his father's eyes when this began has now vanished, replaced by the dull-eyed stare he remembers well. That vacant glaze brought on by the alcohol and the demons that stripped the very life out of the man. He can feel nothing but anger, even hatred for the man he depended on to be strong, and who, along with his mother, let him down. He is seized by a sudden and vicious urge to take his father by the shoulders and shake him like a child. To tell the beaten and broken wreck of a man that he and his mother are to blame for the way their son has turned out.

Yet, the nightmare again and inexplicably veering off-course, he also feels the sudden need to tell his father he is sorry about Lanie.

But why should he apologize? He loved his sister! So cute and funny, and though she was older than he, she worshiped him, often treating him like the older sibling. He wasn't responsible for her death.

Death?

Yes…that was what had happened. He remembers that now and remembers that nothing was ever the same after her death.

But how did she die? Again, he searches his mind, but he can't pull that piece of this puzzling dilemma out of the darkness of his mind. Weird. Surely, if he could remember she had died, he would remember how. Wouldn't he? Yet the manner of her death continues to elude him, and he is even more angered because of it.

He is also so disgusted by his father that he leaves the man to wallow in his own misery. It is only when he looks away from his father that he notices something that leaves him both astounded and frightened.

The entire landscape before his eyes is changing, drastically, the dream or delusion again taking an eerie turn. It has become difficult to see the athletic fields and the school, even harder to see the city beyond, because of the trees that are appearing as if from out of nowhere. In only a few seconds the towering church steeples in the distance are completely hidden by the encroaching trees; quickly after that there is no sign of the school or the athletic fields.

Perplexing as hell though it is, he isn't sorry to see any of it disappear. After Lanie was gone, he remembers, his mother used to drag him to one of those churches and make him pray on his knees. As if that was going to bring his sister back? The school and both the baseball and football fields held no better memories for him. It was on the baseball diamond, near home-plate, when he was just a freshman, that he had charged into a group of seniors. They had angered him by insulting his dead sister, calling them white-trash, and the seniors had beat him senseless. He never forgot that or the insult. He remembers lying there in the dirt, promising himself that he would never endure that kind of bullshit or take another beating like that again.

That he would never be weak like his father had turned out to be.

In hardly more than a few eye-blinks there is nothing to see but trees so tall they are blotting out the sun, creating a sense of false darkness and causing the temperature to drop. As a thin sheen of sweat dries on his skin, he is no longer sitting on the gently sloping rise on the edge of the school grounds, but on a road. A narrow and twisting ribbon of road that disappears through the woods in both directions. Though he doesn't understand what is happening or how he has come to be on this road, he has no trouble recognizing where he is. The old dirt road leads to the levee, and it isn't far to where he lives. Many times, when things at home got to be more than he could bear, he would flee to these woods. But that stopped the night of the fire.

Fire?

Yes…there was a fire, another memory leaping out of the darkness. Was that how Lanie had died? Strangely, he still can't remember that part of it. He can remember that it was a long time after the fire before he saw these woods and this road again.

He gets to his feet, suddenly aware of the tension from his father. He looks down at the elder Moore; the man is pointing at something down the road. His eyes follow his father's pointing finger, a finger that trembles as if from palsy.

What he sees leaves him stunned and, momentarily, unable to get his breath.

In the center of the road and walking towards them is a woman. At first, he thinks it's his mother, but he quickly realizes that he's wrong. This woman has dark hair and wears a long black dress that looks so out of style that it could have come straight out of a time warp. He can't see her face because of the shadows that hide it, but he can hear her laughing. A soft, cruel and insidious laugh that fills him with cold dread. But that isn't the worst of it.

Why does this woman and her laughter seem so familiar to him? To his knowledge, he has never seen this woman before or anyone who even vaguely resembles her.

Perplexed, he glances down at his father, who is now staring up at him with fierce and frightened eyes. The elder Moore grabs his hand, pulls himself to his feet, and stands facing his son. He can feel his father's hot breath in his face and smell the Brut aftershave he always wore.

"You see there, Bradley!" his father shouts, his normally deep voice now high and shrill. "I told you, boy, and told you, but you never believed me! Now it's too late! Way too late!"

Too late for what? *Before Bradley Moore can form the thought into words, the laughter stops, and the woman screams. An ungodly scream unlike any he has ever heard before that rings in his ears seems to shake the ground. The scream lasts only a few seconds, still a dying and chilling echo in his head, when someone—his father?—is yelling in his ear…*

"Wake up, you damned fool…

*

…wake up!"

Bradley Moore's small and piggy blue eyes snapped open. He mentally shook away the last of the dream, or whatever it was, then scowled irritably at the rain beginning to speckle the windshield of his old Chevy Caprice. *What the fuck next?* he thought, then glanced angrily at the man sitting in the passenger seat.

"Don't ever yell in my ear like that again," he growled through clenched teeth, sounding very much like a pissed off Doberman.

"Good thing the road's going straight is all I can say," Robbie Simpson declared. "One hell of a time for you to go to sleep!"

Anger quickly turned into rage that Brad could feel swelling in him. He could smell the foul stench of fear rolling off the man beside him. He would have cranked down the driver's side window if the damn thing would go down. Something had broken inside the door and the window hadn't worked right since right before he was popped on a felony assault charge and became a guest for the second time at one of the maximum-security facilities maintained by the state. That was two years ago; it frankly amazed Brad that the car would even start after sitting parked so long.

And it almost didn't start, both the battery and the starter weak.

"Damn it, just chill the fuck out," Brad snapped. "You're about to lose your shit, and I only closed my eyes for a second." It had seemed no longer than that, anyway.

"How the hell you expect me to chill out?" Robbie countered, his voice as thin and high as he was in stature. Brad had known him for years and often thought, usually after a couple of six-packs, that Robbie was so tall and skinny that it would take two of him to make a shadow. "As if this shit isn't bad enough, you decide to take a nap?" Robbie demanded.

"I wasn't asleep, goddamn it." At least, as far as he could tell, he wasn't asleep. In truth, he would just be fucked if he could say what had happened to him or what had brought on such an episode. The memory of his dead sister? Or maybe the memory of his father and the fire?

The fire…

"What-the-fuck-ever, man! The bottom line here is that we are so screwed!" Robbie shook his head as it left him completely bewildered to find himself in such a spot.

"We'll be fine if you'll just listen to me and fucking relax," Brad growled, his eyes back on the road again. In addition to the rain, now it was getting dark, the gray and dingy light of the cloudy April evening all but gone. With only one headlight that still worked, Brad knew he was driving his old heap along a narrow and twisting road and through a densely wooded area much faster than was safe. The road beneath the car's nearly bald tires was dirt and rough as hell. *Damn it, we've got to get this done and get the hell out of here before this road turns into a fucking nightmare. Too bad Robbie's truck wasn't better suited for this run.*

"All that goddamn blood," Robbie said, his voice now a low and anguished moan. "Makes me sick to my stomach just to think about it."

Then quit thinking about it, dumb ass. "We can get rid of the blood," Brad said, leaning heavily on *"we."* He swerved around a pot-hole, the tires nearly losing their grip, the Caprice veering dangerously close to a tree, and said, "Just as we're getting rid of her now."

"That's the point, damn it!" Robbie countered, his voice now so shrill that it cracked. "I could've took her ass back across the river to Memphis and dropped her off on the damn street corner where I found her! Simple and clean, no drama! But now, thanks to you, we got a dead bitch in the trunk!" He glanced at Brad, who could almost feel his eyes and the feral fear coming off the man. "You and your damn temper, and less than twenty-four hours on the outside! At least the last time you didn't kill anyone. I should've just drove on this morning and left you standing there at the fucking gate."

Brad shot him a look. *But you didn't dare do that because I would've hunted your ass down and you know it.* "What the hell was I supposed to do?" he demanded, his voice now hot and rising. "Let the bitch run off with every fucking dollar we could scrape together?"

"She ran because you scared the hell out of her," Robbie snapped.

Brad grunted a mirthless, scoffing laugh. "Yeah, right," he drawled. "Damn bitch was up to no good from the start."

"You told me on the trip from the prison that you wanted something to eat, a cold beer, and some pussy—in that order," Robbie insisted. "So, I try to accommodate you. But as soon as I walk in with her, you pull that fucking knife of yours and tell her you'll cut her tits off if she tries anything. Goddamn, Brad, who the fuck wouldn't run?"

"Letting her know I wasn't going to put up with any bullshit," Brad growled. "Besides, she didn't try to run before she had the money, did she? Hell, no! She waits until she has it in her purse—before she even takes a stitch off—and then she's running for the backdoor. No way in hell was she getting away with that shit." He almost caught her on the back porch, where she stopped long enough to pull off her heels, his hand missing her arm by inches. Then she was running like a damn deer toward the trees at the back of his property. If not for the way she stumbled on something in the grass and fell ass over end she might have gotten away, but he caught her. With her screaming her head off—like someone was going to hear the dumb bitch all the way out there in the sticks? —he had grabbed her by the hair, yanked her to her feet, and marched her ass back to the house.

"You didn't have to kill her, though," Robbie groused, his voice again low and raw. "I mean, hell, you got what you wanted. Hell, we both did."

Damn right we did. Brad had made sure the bitch kept her end of the deal. Many times, she did it for free.

"What the hell was the point in killing her?" Robbie pressed.

Brad sighed, beyond angered. He was getting tired of the whiner's bullshit. "I didn't hear you complaining or asking questions all the time you had her bent over the arm of the couch and grunting like a damn pig. I say again—what else was I supposed to do? Let the bitch walk after we finished with her, so she go straight to the cops? Don't know about you, asshole, but I sure as shit don't need a third strike."

A long moment of pregnant silence, then, "No…I guess you couldn't do anything else." Robbie's voice was now heavy and sulky.

"No, I damn well guess I couldn't."

"Not after you started cutting on her," Robbie drawled.

"Taught the bitch what it means to cross me."

"I mean, hell, after you cut off her finger, then started peeling the skin off her back like you were field-dressing a buck…well, no going back after that."

Brad took his eyes away from the road long enough to glare at Robbie, a stare hot enough to burn. Robbie refused to meet his stare, his own eyes fixed straight ahead out the windshield. Brad realized, and with no surprise, that he was going to have to keep an eye on Robbie. Brad had considered him a friend for years and owed Robbie more than a few favors. Robbie had stayed at his place, keeping an eye on his property and his old Caprice, until his release. Had even held on to some money for him.

None of which changed the fact that the skinny dumb fuck and his nervously bobbing Adam's Apple could easily get them both sent straight to death row at Tucker. And Brad was having none of that. *Not over some lousy whore no one's going to miss or some scared asshole who needs to grow a fucking pair of balls.*

*

There was only silence between them the rest of the way. Brad kept driving through the steady light rain until the road simply ended in a small clearing in the middle of nowhere. Brad switched off the car's one headlight, plunging them into inky darkness. He thought about it, then switched off the engine, hoping it would start again. He pushed open the door, the dome light blinking on, and got out of the car. The muddy and fishy smell of the Mississippi River hung heavy and rank on the lightly gusting wind. He glanced back inside the car at Robbie, who still sat in the passenger seat like a rock. *Goddamn gutless fuck...*

"Come on, damn it, get your ass out and help with this," he snarled.

Robbie opened the door and got out, moving like he was a hundred years old. By the dim glow of the dome light, Brad watched him holding the car's door with both hands as if afraid to let go, his head turning this way and that.

"For fuck's sake, Brad," he breathed. "You know where we are?"

Brad scowled. "Goddamn, you just now figured it out?" The asshole had to be even more rattled than he had first thought.

"Now I know you've lost your mind," Robbie said, now sounding like he couldn't get his breath at all. "Man, you said it yourself, no one in their right mind comes out here at night."

"Exactly why we're here," Brad drawled, closing the driver's side door. It had been years since he had been to the area; he had almost missed the turn off to the dirt road from the county two-lane. Thankfully, the old and rusting steel gate hidden just inside the trees, a gate usually closed and locked, was open. Created back in the early-70's so the Corp of Engineers could inspect an extended section of the levee along the Mississippi River, the dirt road had no name. Not an official name that appeared on any map.

There was a second, smaller clearing, a break in the dark wall of trees just beyond the one in which he had stopped the car. Brad knew this second clearing to be one of the many long and narrow bar-ditch ponds, from which those building the levee had excavated the dirt. Except for that ditch and the others scarring the landscape, there was nothing for miles but the river and the levee and a veritable wilderness. The perfect place to dump garbage that needed to stay hidden. Brad judged that, by the time anyone found the bitch in the trunk—*if anyone does find her*—she would be nothing but bones and scattered to hell and back by the coyotes. Better than throwing her ass in the river, the first option to cross Brad's mind, and hoping she didn't wash ashore somewhere downstream.

"I don't know about this," Robbie said in a near whisper. "The way I hear it, even the horny kids stay the fuck away from here at night, and I got no problem believing it, either. I came out here a couple of times while you were inside, just to see the place, and it was just plain spooky as fuck—and I was here the middle of the afternoon both times."

Wish now I'd never told you the fucking story of this place. It was his father who had first told Brad about the young woman, the wife of one of the men working to make the road, who had brought her husband lunch one day and died in a freak accident when a tree fell the wrong way. Brad's father said there were many who believed it to be no accident, and that the spirit of the dead woman still wandered these woods, looking for her husband and her revenge. His father also said there were a few who claimed they had heard a woman's fiendish laughter and a shrill scream. It was the scream that had become legend among locals, mostly heard around noontime when the woman died, though a few others, according to his father, had heard it at other times as well, even at night. Those who had claimed to hear the scream swore the sound of it seemed to fill the woods.

Brad had always thought it possible that some bitch had died out here. Shit, it seemed likely enough. Even possible that it may have been intentional for whatever reason. It was the rest of the story that he had never believed. Even as a ten-year old, when he had first heard the story from his old man, Brad had dismissed the idea of a vengeful and laughing and screaming spirit as a load of bullshit. He had been here many times and had yet to hear either fiendish laughter or a scream. Had never once even felt spooked.

Not until a few minutes ago, anyway. Whatever the hell that was that had happened to him, though he would never admit it to a living soul, had spooked him.

But to hell with that. Whatever the hell had happened to him had nothing to do with a bullshit story told by a drunken father, who managed to burn the house down one night when he passed out with a lit cigarette, killing himself and Brad's mother. Nothing but a drunk, herself, his mother, also passed out at the time of the blaze. His T-shirt on fire and most of his hair singed away, Brad had barely escaped with his life.

The memory of his parents and the deadly fire suddenly left Brad feeling unsettled again, but he quickly shut down the feeling. No time for shit like that. Ignoring Robbie, he stepped to the back of the car and opened the trunk. The dead hooker…what was left of her…lay wrapped like a bloody enchilada in an old shower curtain.

"Brad…we need to get the fuck away from here," Robbie said, speaking as if his voice was somehow stuck in his throat.

Brad stifled an irritated sigh, glanced around the edge of the raised trunk lid, and regarded Robbie disgustedly. The asshole had only been afraid before; now he sounded as terrified as some kid in his bed at night and eyeing the closet door.

"Man, I mean it," Robbie went on, apparently oblivious to the near murderous stare he was getting from Brad. "We need to leave here, now. Look, I never said anything about this until now because I didn't want to sound like some pussy…but the last time I was here?" He paused, drawing in an audible breath, then said, "I heard that fucking scream you mentioned. I swear I did—I wasn't twenty yards away from this very spot and I heard it through the woods back toward the county road. It was a woman screaming, and it only lasted a few seconds…but it was the worst thing I've ever heard. Like nothing that could be alive."

Brad had heard enough of this bullshit. He stepped around the back of the car and stood facing Robbie, his hands on his hips. "Bring your ass back here and help with this," he said in his most threatening voice. The voice that never failed to get an asshole's attention. "I'm not even going to say it twice, either."

Robbie's head dropped and, reluctantly, he started toward the back of the car. Once he was moving, Brad stepped back to the trunk, reached inside and, grunting with the effort, hauled the woman out, and dropped her on the ground like a bag of sand.

It gave him a rather nasty start when the

bitch groaned softly at his feet, the shower curtain crackling a bit as if she was moving.

"Well, kiss my ass," he murmured so softly that Robbie never heard the words. Brad, after the way he had carved her ass up like a Thanksgiving turkey, thought for sure the bitch was dead long before he hauled her out of the house and loaded her into the trunk. No matter. Even if she was still alive, it wouldn't be for long, as he wasn't finished with her yet. Ignoring her for the moment, he fumbled inside the trunk, took out a mag-light and a black garbage bag, into which he had stuffed the bitch's clothes, purse, heels, and her severed finger. When Robbie finally came around the back of the car, Brad handed him both the light and the bag.

"Take that and come on," he said, stooping to pick the woman up. As he stood up with her, she moaned again and mumbled something.

Robbie, only a few steps away, breathed, "Jesus-fucking-Christ." He took a step back, again peering into the darkness in every direction. "She can't be still alive. Man, what the fuck is going on here?"

"Don't start that shit again," Brad warned, hoisting up his burden and slinging her over one shoulder. "Just turn that light on and start walking."

"Walking where?"

"Straight out from the car, dipshit, until you come to the ditch, then follow it to the right." The levee and the river beyond it was to the left of the ditch. What Brad had in mind was to reach the far end of the ditch, a couple of hundred yards away, then cut sharply back into the deep woods another couple of hundred. He remembered from one of his own and last forays into these woods that there was a shallow ravine hidden beneath a thicket of tangled underbrush and briars. Once he and Robbie reached that spot…

…well, he had his knife, and there was also a hacksaw and a hammer in the garbage bag. Even if someone found her, good luck trying to identify a bitch with no head or fingers or teeth. The only real problems facing him, as Brad saw it, was time and the rain and Robbie.

The asshole's going to freak when I start smashing the bitch's teeth out.

*

It was slow going. Robbie was in no hurry, shambling along like they had all night. Yet Brad couldn't complain; his load had gotten heavy in a hurry and he was having a hell of a time with it. Too many cigarettes and idle hours spent in front of a TV…in between stints inside, of course. His breathing was harsh and heavy long before he and Robbie made it to the end of the ditch. There he stopped long enough to shift his burden to his other shoulder, then trudged on, trailing after Robbie as he cut back into the woods. The lightly falling rain wasn't helping, the leaves underfoot just wet enough to make footing treacherous, and the damn shower curtain was slippery and tough to hold on to.

The weird thing about it was that Brad was almost sure the bitch wrapped in the shower curtain was moving. Not much, but enough to suggest she was still alive. But that was fucking crazy! She had to be dead by now! At one point, he thought he heard a groan from her, but he quickly dismissed that as the thump of his pulse in his temples.

Got to wrap this up and get out of here before that road's impassible...

Robbie, Brad realized, was following a trail. Not much of one, but a trail all the same, and one Brad didn't remember. Fuck it. They were moving deeper into the woods and going, roughly, in the direction Brad wanted to go. By the time he spotted the ravine and thicket he remembered, Brad was completely out of breath and wheezing heavily. He grunted at Robbie, getting his attention, then dropped his load on the ground.

This time, there was a groan he heard clearly from within the folds of opaque plastic. *What fuck's keeping the bitch alive?*

"This the place?" Robbie asked, shining

the light this way and that.

At first, still out of breath, Brad could only nod, though he wanted to slap the piss out of the stupid fuck for waving the light around. He was sure there was no one around, but why take stupid chances now? He stepped close enough to Robbie to yank the light from his hand and aimed the beam at the thicket.

"In there," Brad rasped. "But I can do that." *Once I'm finished with her ass.* "Just give me a minute to get my breath back."

"Fine," Robbie said. "Do it yourself." He dropped the garbage bag and started walking away, retracing their steps along the trail back toward the ditch.

"The fuck you think you're going?" Brad demanded.

"Away from you and here," Robbie retorted, spitting the words over his shoulder as he kept walking. There was a distinct note of finality in his voice.

"Just walk away? Just like that?"

"Damn right," Robbie shot back, wheeling around to face Brad. "I want nothing else to do with this fucking mess. You cut her up and killed her, so you can take care of it the best way you can—and if I never see your ass again, that suits the fuck out of me."

That, and the fact that the key was in the Caprice's ignition, clenched it, sealing the dumb fuck's fate. Brad shifted the light to his left hand, his right reaching for a back pocket of his jeans. "Hey, damn it, wait a minute," he said, stepping quickly toward Robbie, shining the beam of light in the man's face.

"What?" Robbie demanded, standing his ground, one hand shielding his eyes.

"This, motherfucker," Brad snarled, then dropped the flashlight and lunged at Robbie. In Brad's right hand was his folding knife, the blade open and locked in place.

Either Robbie never saw the knife because Brad had momentarily blinded him with the light or because he never suspected what was coming. The dumb ass just stood there. Brad drove the knife into his belly just under the navel, a warm gush of blood splashing his hand, and ripped up with it. The blade parted flesh like passing through butter until it hit bone. Brad's friend when he walked out of prison that morning, now the most dangerous man on earth to him, made no sound beyond a grunt and a soft expulsion of breath as his body sagged and swayed. Then he toppled over backward, the knife pulling free.

Brad stood over him, but Robbie didn't move or make another sound. Not convinced, Brad grabbed up the light and centred the beam on Robbie's face. The man's eyes were open, already turning glassy. There were several loops of intestines poking out of the gaping wound in his belly. Just to be sure, Brad slashed open his throat. There was more blood, but not the spray he had anticipated. Finally satisfied, he wiped his knife and hand on Robbie's shirt and folded the knife's blade closed.

Behind him, as he returned the knife to his back pocket, the woman groaned again.

Brad could only shake his head, then he glanced at Robbie. "Looks like she was a lot tougher than you were…and you left me no other choice, either." And, like the woman, no one was likely to miss the dumb fuck. He wasn't from the area; Brad had been his only real friend and he had no family. None that he had ever mentioned. Brad turned back to the woman.

The rain was picking up, the splatter of the cold drops a steady and sibilant rhythm. No time, Brad realized, to dick around with getting either of them into the thicket or fixing things so that identifying them was next to impossible. Where they lay was good enough. It would have to be. Brad found the garbage bag, heaved it into the darkness, then grabbed a flap of the shower curtain and rolled the woman out of it. Again, to Brad's amazement, she moaned, then mumbled something he couldn't make out. It was like she was stirring awake from a nap.

Fuck her. No way in hell will she ever walk out of here. Brad wadded up the shower curtain and, with it under one arm, started back to his car.

He would take the shower curtain home

and dispose of it there. Burn it, maybe, along with the clothes he had on and several other things from the house. Provided he could bring himself to do it that way. There was nothing he hated more than a fire of any kind. But, one way or another, he would get rid of everything he had to, including Robbie's pickup. Then he would give his place a good scrubbing. It would take him most of the night—like he had anything more important to do? —but there would be no trace left that either of those he left on the ground had ever been there. After that…

Damn, I could use a cold beer. There was most of a twelve-pack Robbie had bought in the fridge at home. *And, this time, I don't have to share it with a gutless fuck.*

*

It took only a few minutes for him to find his way back to the ditch. He was soaked to the skin, briar-scratched, and ready to see the last of this damn place. He had just turned in the direction of his car, wondering if the damn thing would start, when…

…a bright flash of orange and red that seemed to light up the woods stopped him in his tracks. Even after the initial flash had passed there remained a source of intense and flickering light. It took only a moment for him to realize that what he was seeing was a fire. And that it seemed to be coming from where he had parked his Caprice.

Completely bewildered, the reflection of the flames dancing in his eyes and an uneasy feeling crawling up his throat from the pit of his stomach, Brad set off at a run toward the source of the fire.

He had run only a few yards when he slipped in the wet leaves, both feet flying out from under him, and he crashed to the ground.

"Fuck," he mouthed, pushing himself up on his hands. Once back on his feet, he checked himself as best he could. His right kneecap had struck something hard, maybe an exposed root; otherwise he seemed unhurt. His kneecap was hurting like a bitch; he could only hope the knee didn't start swelling and get stiff. He tested the knee and found it would take his weight with no additional pain. *Lucky I didn't break my fucking leg.* He looked up, staring in the direction he had been running. That was when he noticed that...

What the fuck?

If it had been his old Caprice that was burning, and he was reasonably sure it was, then what the fuck had happened to the fire? There was no glow of flames through the trees ahead of him, only darkness as black as the devil's heart. He picked up his light—*a fucking miracle it's still working after that tumble I took*—but even its bright beam seemed to penetrate the darkness only a few yards. How could the Caprice have burned out so fast? There should have at least been glowing pinpoints of hot spots and dying flames...but there was only the darkness.

Despite himself, a shiver, like a sliver of ice, sliced through him. Hard on the heels of that was a second sensation, one he had felt once before when his sister died, a feeling so strong and gripping that he would swear he could hear it like a voice in his head, taunting him.

Remember me, motherfucker?

Yeah, I remember the feeling of regret. It was as sour and empty as he remembered. But why was he feeling it now? What the hell did he have to regret? He did what he had to do. He had always done what he had to.

But, right now, that was beside the point. The point was that something really fucked up was happening and had been since he drove into these woods. But what was it? Beyond the simple fact that something, obviously, had to be fucking with his head, he didn't have a clue.

No time for this shit! Did he still have a car or not? He was still pondering that question, his free hand rubbing at his sore knee when...

...the sound of distant laughter reached him. A woman's laughter, soft and melodic like a song and fading to silence after only a few seconds. It was coming from the direction where he had left Robbie and the hooker.

"You and your damned temper," Robbie's

voice said in his head, *"and less than twenty-four hours on the outside. At least you didn't kill anyone the last time."*

And just look at what you've gone and done this time...damned crazy bastard.

Yeah, I killed them both—so what?

Who the fuck am I trying to kid? In truth, even if he tried, he couldn't bring himself to give a fuck about the hooker. Nothing but a skank. But Robbie...

*That's right, asshole. Your best friend—hell, your **only** friend! Who else called you every chance he got when you were inside? Who wrote you letters and bothered to come see you? The only person who had time for you—and how many of those have you known since your sister died? Answer that one, if you can.*

Knock it off, goddamn it. Stop acting like your damned weak-minded father and start thinking about getting the fuck out of here!

Then the sound of laughter drifted to him again.

Only this time it was the fiendish sound of sinister mirth he had heard when he blanked out behind the wheel...and it was much closer now, as if the bitch was trailing him. As it had before, the sound faded after only a few seconds.

It had to be the hooker, but was that even possible? Even if the bitch was still alive and able to make a sound, she would be screaming, not laughing.

Screaming? Goddamn…what if it really isn't her but some other bitch?

Like the one dear-old drunken daddy told you about?

A possibility he refused to contemplate; he quickly pushed the idea from his mind. This place and the situation he found himself in was getting to him. Not like him at all; nothing ever got to him or spooked him to such an extent.

Then he heard the laugher for the third time. It was even closer now. Instinctively, his hand reached for his knife in his back pocket. Despite the fear rising in him, roiling and twisting in him like a nest of snakes, he could feel the old and familiar burn of rage in his belly. *Just show yourself, whoever the fuck you are, and I'll take away any reason you have to laugh.*

But nothing appeared in the range of his light and, as it had before, the sound of laughter faded as quickly as it came. After that there was only the sound of…

…nothing. The woods were still and silent, and eerily so.

When had it stopped raining? He looked up, amazed to see a sky filled with stars. There was even a sliver of a buttery-yellow moon visible through the trees, just beginning to rise. The icy slash of fear he had felt before cut into him again.

He found the shower curtain where he had dropped it, decided to hell with it, and shone his light in the direction he had seen the fire…

…and froze without taking a step. It felt like his eyes were about to pop out of his head.

In the beam of his light was a thicket of brush and briars nearly as tall as he was, and it stretched as far as his light could reach in both directions. It looked like a wall—was a damned wall, and it hadn't been there before. He and Robbie hadn't passed through anything like this on the way in. Thinking he may have gotten turned around and was facing the wrong way, he shone his light behind him…

…and there he found a second wall of brush and thorns, and one that hadn't been there before, either. He was hemmed in as if he had walked into a trap. The worst of it was that there didn't seem to be a way out. Not without the thorns—some of the damned things looked to be an inch or more long! —cutting him to pieces. He was still pondering this daunting and frightening new predicament when…

…a new sound reached him. A faint, far-away sound that seemed to be coming from every direction at once. His eyes narrowed, his expression one of complete bewilderment.

Church bells? Yeah…the slow tolling of church bells. Much like the forlorn sound of bells he had heard at the end of his sister's funeral service as the pall-bearers carried her coffin from the church to the waiting hearse.

But that was impossible! The nearest church was miles away in town!

Yet the bells kept ringing, the sound chilling him to his very soul, and his nerve finally deserted him in a rush.

Head lowered, again facing the moon and the direction in which he thought—hoped, as nothing looked familiar to him—he had parked his car, he crashed into the wall of brush and thorns like a charging bull. The thicket seemed to swallow him, the briars tearing at his clothes and ripping into his flesh. It felt like hundreds of wasps were stinging him from head to foot. Still, in something very close to a panic, the sound of the bells still ringing softly in his ears, he pawed his way through it, the cuts and slashes on his hands and arms and legs burning like fire.

Fire!

The memory of the fire, of stumbling through the smoke and flames, flashed through his mind. The image made him groan in fear, but that quickly turned into a snarl of animal-like fury; he bulled his way forward. The bells were still tolling, but faster now; it was like a pounding in his head that seemed in perfect cadence with his pulse.

Goddamn it, is there no end to these fucking vines and thorns? He seemed to be making little progress. At most, gaining a few inches at a time, if that. He began to wonder if he was going to make it out of there. *A briar thicket! Of all the bullshit things!*

"We need to leave here, now. Look I never said anything about this until now because I don't want to sound like some pussy…but the last time I was here?" A pause, a drawn breath, then, *"I heard that fucking scream you mentioned. I swear I did—I wasn't twenty yards away from this very spot and I heard it through the woods back toward the county road. It was a woman screaming, and it only lasted a few seconds…but it was the worst thing I've ever heard. Like nothing that could be alive."*

"Fuck that shit, Robbie," he mumbled in a low, snarling hiss. He still had the light, but he had lost his knife; it had slipped from his bloody fingers. That made him the maddest he had been so far. That knife had meant more to him than most people he had known!

"Fuck you…fuck this—***FUCK ALL THIS SHIT!***" The sound of the bells still ringing in his head, faster and faster, his breathing coming in harsh and laboured barks, he summoned the last bit of resolve and strength he possessed. The briars tore at his jeans and shirt with renewed fury, further slashing his already bleeding flesh.

But he was now gaining ground. Not mere inches, but feet and yards, one massive and determined step after another. On and on…

Finally, hope surged in him when he spied what looked like an opening in the moonlight just ahead of him. Grunting with the effort, he crashed out of the thicket, stood just beyond it a few seconds, swaying on his feet, then dropped to his knees, completely exhausted. The taste of his own blood on his lips, he slumped to the ground and rolled onto his back.

He had no idea how long he lay there on the ground, eyes closed, his breathing slowly returning to normal. The entire front of his body from head to foot felt raw as if he had been skinned. Despite the burn of pain, he could feel the warm seep of blood from what had to be hundreds of deep scratches and cuts.

Man, one of those cold beers at home would go down so good right now.

When he finally opened his eyes, he was surprised to see light creeping into the sky. Dawn had come and gone and soon would come the sun. Had it taken that long to paw his way out of the thicket? Most of the night?

Fuck it. The important thing was that he was out of the briars. He sat up, grimacing at the pain that seemed to be coming from every part of his body.

Only then did he become aware of his surroundings. He sat on the edge of a clearing, not unlike the one where he had parked his car. The only difference was that there were nothing but leaves on the ground where he parked; now there was a soft bed of green and vibrant grass beneath him. He looked around, knowing it was pointless, and wasn't surprised to see no sign of his car. Yet what met his eyes was, perhaps, the most perplexing thing he had seen so far.

He had stumbled out of the thicket into a children's park and, stranger still, one he had been to before. He recognized the tall metal slide with the bright fire-engine red steps and the monkey bars. Recognized the metal-framed swing set and brightly coloured roundabout, now still and silent, no children pushing it and others riding it.

Yet he wasn't alone and, he realized in a foggy, dream-like way, he could no longer hear the tolling bells. The only sounds were the ratcheting squeals of the chains from one of the swings and the soft childish laughter from the girl riding it. Her hair was the color of oranges, her freckled arms and the pale skin of her face ripe with fresh sunburn.

My God, it can't be…

He stood up slowly, leaving what understanding he still possessed on the ground. He walked slowly toward the girl, mindful of how he must look slashed and cut as he was and not wanting to scare her away. As if suddenly aware of his presence, the girl stopped swinging and looked around at him.

"Lanie," he whispered, his knees going a little weak when she smiled. The smile that he would never forget. She looked the way she did the last time he saw her when she was ten and he was seven. Even wearing the same clothes she had on the day she died. She reached for one of the chains of the swing next to her.

"Sit with me, Braddie," she whispered, calling him by the nickname only she had ever used. "Come, while there's still time."

He approached her hesitantly, glancing at the swing in which she wanted him to sit. It seemed so incredible and impossible, yet so good at the same time to see her, and to see her as she was now, as she had been. It was almost hypnotic watching the way the sun danced and shone golden in her hair. Nonetheless, he couldn't bring himself to sit beside her. She was dead, he understood that, and he had missed her terribly, but there was still an aura of innocence about her; he feared he would somehow taint that if he got too close to her. Lanie read his expression perfectly; understanding filled her blue eyes.

"It's okay, Braddie. I can't stay very long, anyway." A look of sadness appeared in her eyes, and her smile vanished. "Oh, Braddie, there was always so much good in you and I never stopped hoping that you would let it out and not let all the bad things make you so bitter and angry and to do all the things you've done."

Brad was trembling visibly all over. He wanted to tell her why he had turned out the way he had, but his voice had deserted him, and it was partly because what had happened to her had suddenly appeared in his mind's eye. It was like a vicious blow to the head. He had never forgotten what had happened to her; he knew that now and knew he would never forget it. He just didn't let himself think about it.

She was hit by a car. They had been at the park—this very park—and were walking home when an old Gran Torino, even more of a piece of junk than his Caprice, had roared up from out of nowhere. He and Lanie were cutting up, having some fun with each other, and he had darted playfully into the street away from her. Lanie saw what was coming, had run into the street and pushed him toward the sidewalk an instant before the Torino crashed into her, rolling over her. She was dead before he could crawl to her crushed body. The only part after that he couldn't remember was how long he had sat there in the street, crying and holding her bloody hand. The next thing he did remember clearly was his father wailing out his grief and punching one of the living room walls until the knuckles of both hands were bleeding. Long after the man died in the fire, no matter if Brad was awake or asleep, he could hear his father moaning Lanie's name over and over again in a whiskey-slurred whimper.

"I wish it had been me that day," he finally murmured. It was all he could think of to say and, as he learned later, it was a sentiment he had shared with his father. His mother also, but it was his father who was the most vocal about it. When he wasn't hitting the bottle, he was hitting Brad's mother and yelling at her. *"Should have aborted his ass like I told you to do time after time!"* he would shout in his liquor and grief fueled rages. *"Look at all the trouble you would've saved us if only you'd listened to me!"* She willingly took the abuse, and Brad never once heard the woman disagree with anything his father said.

But all of that was just the beginning of what had shaped and made him. For the first time in years he felt an overwhelming need to explain himself, but he suspected that Lanie already knew most, if not all the reasons, and he could think of nothing to say that wouldn't make it sound like he was blaming her—and she the only one truly blameless. Was it her fault that their parents went to pieces and made his life a living hell until the day they died? Was it her fault that the driver of the Torino had fled the scene as if he had hit nothing more important than a stray dog? Was it her fault that the fucking cops never found the murdering asshole because they had never tried very hard? Was it Lanie's fault that he trusted no one and would never forget those insults in school or the beating he had taken on the baseball field?

"I couldn't let that car hit you, Braddie," Lanie whispered. "But that doesn't really matter now because it's too late for you, and all you can do now is run. You've got to run because now she's looking for you."

Brad's eyes narrowed. "She who is looking for me?"

"Braddie, you know who I mean. You refused to take seriously all these years what dad told you, but you can't afford to do that anymore. She's real, she's here, and you've killed here, where she lives, and she always comes for the wicked and evil, and she's coming for you."

As if to punctuate Lanie's words, he again heard the cruel and insidious laughter that had seemed to be following him through the woods. Only now it was the closest it had been so far. By the sound of it, the bitch—*can it really be the one the old man told me about? Can that be anything but a drunk trying to scare the piss out of me just to make me as miserable as he was?* —was somewhere just beyond the edge of the clearing.

This time the laughter didn't fade to silence after a few seconds, but continued, growing louder and more sinister.

"Run, Braddie, run!" Lanie shouted, jumping free of the swing. Then she was running toward the edge of the clearing at a point between him and the laughter. "Run and don't look back!" She had reached the trees when she glanced back over her shoulder. "Whatever you do," she yelled a split second before she vanished into the trees, "don't look her straight in the face!"

No more than a second after that Brad was running in the opposite direction, the sound of the laughter drawing even closer. As he thrashed through the trees, thankful there was no thicket and briars this time, he could still hardly believe the story his father told him—to say nothing of what Robbie had said at the car—was all true.

Had to be true! Something was and had been pursuing him and screwing with him since he drove into these woods. But, more than that, Lanie had clearly believed there was something evil here, and she was the one person on earth that he had trusted completely.

So he ran as he had never run before.

*

The trees were large and close together, the underbrush thick, but he had little trouble getting through it. The sound of the laughter never seemed very far behind him. He had run, perhaps, a hundred yards when he spied what appeared to be yet another opening in the woods ahead of him and slightly to his right. Should he risk going there? What if it was where he had parked his car? Provided there was a car still waiting for him. He wasn't sure of anything, and nothing about the woods looked the least bit familiar to him, even in the daylight.

It was like he had never seen these fucking woods before!

In the end, because if he still had a car and it was parked in the clearing ahead of him, he could get out of these woods a lot faster that way than he ever could on foot.

He crashed out of the trees into the clearing. No sign of his car, but what he saw stopped him cold. Again, surprise overwhelmed him, his eyes again bulging in their sockets.

There was a lake in the clearing, the shoreline facing him pebbled. A boat, an aluminium flat-bottom—a fourteen-footer by the look of it—bobbed in the water at a small wooden dock. On the other side of the lake was a white two-story house and with green trim and a green-tiled roof. Brad stared at, first the lake, then the house in complete disbelief.

The Dawson place? How the fuck can I be here? This damn place is all the way on the other side of town, for fuck's sake!

He knew the place well, Dan and Christine Dawson the foster family that took him in after his parents died. It wasn't bad at first. No Little House on the Prairie, but not that bad. Not until he discovered that he and the Dawson's son, Tim, had a strong and mutual dislike of each other. Tim, two years older and a jock in school and all full of himself, always seemed to be on his ass about one thing or another. There had been several loud arguments between the boys and they had come to blows on a few occasions. None of which proved all that serious or threatened to end Brad's stay with the family. Not until one day just after his sixteenth birthday when Tim jumped him, accusing him of keying the side of his car. Brad never went near the asshole's car, but when the bastard swung on him, the fight was on and it ended with Tim beaten and bloody on the ground. That was the end of it and, knowing that Dan and

Christine would never listen to him and not wanting to wait around for the hammer to fall or to go back into the system, Brad simply took off. Convinced he could make it on his own and, for a while, he did.

Until his old nemesis—trouble—found him again. It would always find him eventually; there was no way to avoid it, a lesson he had learned that day on the baseball diamond. Another hard lesson he had learned early on was that there was no one left on the face of the earth that gave a fuck about him. The only one who ever did was Lanie.

"And me," said a voice from right beside him.

"Fuck!" Brad yelped and spun around to find...

...*holy fucking shit!*

"I gave a fuck," Robbie Simpson said, his glassy and dead eyes fixed on the lake. "But all it got me was dead."

Brad backed away from the corpse standing there so casually beside him as if admiring the view. Brad had seen some sights—hell, he had created most of them! —but the one he now faced left him feeling faintly sick to his stomach.

Robbie couldn't have been dead for more than a few hours, and yet it seemed that decay had already set in. His face had assumed a putrid shade of blueish-grey, his sunken eyes ringed with purple. From the gash in his throat and covering the front of his shirt was what looked like dried black tar, instead of blood. Ropes of blackened intestines hung obscenely from the gaping hole in his belly. He was covered with ugly green and blue flies, hundreds of the damn things feasting on and buzzing in and out of both wounds. And the stench...

It was all Brad could do to keep from gagging.

"You didn't have to do this to me, you know," Robbie said, very matter-of-factly. Then, for the first time since he had appeared, he fixed his dead eyes on Brad. "But I'm not here for revenge, so don't worry about that. Trust me when I say you've already got someone hot on your ass for revenge and, believe it or not, I'm trying to save you."

"Trying to save me," Brad murmured in a guarded monotone. He was about to speak again when he realized that he could no longer hear the insidious laughter that had followed since he left Lanie and the park. Had the laughter stopped when he entered this new clearing? A clearing and all it contained that simply couldn't be here in this place? He had no way of knowing for sure when the laughter stopped. He wasn't sure of anything. He swallowed, still fighting not to gag on the horrid stench of corruption, and said, "After what I did to you, tell me why I should believe you."

"Because it's true," Robbie replied, his dead eyes locked with Brad's. "Damn it, Brad, you've got to trust somebody and, right now, I'm all you've got."

"Okay, then tell me what the fuck is happening." Brad pointed toward the house. "How can that be here? And the lake?"

"And the park where you found Lanie?" Robbie interrupted. "The church bells?"

"And those damn thickets!" Brad added, holding up his arms and glaring at the cuts and streaks of dried blood. At least that part of it was real enough. Still, he was again locked in a struggle to control his anger. This—all of this—was bullshit, and he was sick of it.

"She's toying with you," Robbie said. "Fucking with your head. Her way of knocking down your resistance. That makes it easier for her to get to you."

"How the fuck do I get out of here?" Brad demanded.

Robbie turned slightly and pointed toward the woods to his left. "That way," he said. "It's a good four, maybe five hundred yards, but if you go straight and not in this circle you've been going in since you left me, you'll come to your car."

"Meaning the damn thing's still there?"

"There was no fire. Like I said, she's been fucking with you this whole time."

"Who is she, goddamn it?"

"I don't know her name, but she's the woman who died here in that accident back in the 70's. She's dark-haired, dark-eyed, and she's wearing a long black dress...and she's one pissed off bitch and more evil than anything you've ever come across."

Brad thought back to the dream or hallucination or whatever the fuck that was that came over him soon after he drove off the county two-lane and entered the woods. The dark-haired woman in the dark dress, walking up the center of the dirt road toward and he and his father. No doubt the very bitch Robbie had just described. Brad tried and failed to stop the shiver that rippled through him. If not confronted with so much weird shit and proof he couldn't dispute, he would have never thought something like this was possible.

"So, if I were you," Robbie was saying, "I'd stop stalling around and asking questions and get the fuck out of here."

"No, fuck him!" shouted a new voice. "Let her have his sorry ass!"

Again, Brad was jarred by surprise, though far back in a dark recess of his mind he had to wonder how anything could still surprise him at this point. His head jerked toward the woods behind where he and Robbie stood. And there...

...her long blonde hair matted with blood and her face streaked with it, was the naked and nearly skinned hooker shambling awkwardly toward them. She could have been a walking pile of mulch from all the leaves stuck to her mutilated body and clinging in her hair. Brad, the thought coming to him completely unbidden, remembered that she had called herself Evie.

"You deserve nothing less than a fate worse than death for what you did to me," she declared, then her stare flicked from Brad to Robbie. "Like the fate he's going to suffer."

"Tell me she's not alive," Brad mumbled to Robbie, remembering how the hooker had been moving and moaning at the car and after he had dumped her in the woods.

"She's dead, all right," Robbie said. "The bitch in black just got to her soon after we got to these fucking woods, and now she's helping her. Don't worry about this one, though. I'll deal with her, and the other one, if she shows, and buy you some time, so get going."

Brad could only stare at Robbie's dead and ghastly face. *Goddamn, he really is trying to help me... and I killed the poor dumb fuck.*

"One thing, though," Robbie said, moving resolutely toward the still advancing corpse of the hooker. "What Lanie said about looking the bitch in black in the face? Remember that, and one other thing, too. If you do look her in the face and she screams? Might as well kiss your ass good-bye because you'll soon be one of us."

Brad was running when he reached the woods. He heard the grunts and shrieks of what sounded like a fierce struggle behind him, but that was all he heard. He never looked back and, quickly, all he could hear was the pound of his running feet and his heart thundering in his chest.

***

The further he ran the blacker the woods became until, finally, he realized that what had seemed like the light of day was still the dark of night. It was also raining again; he felt as if he had passed through some portal from the terrifying world he had stumbled into and back into the one he had left. With both the rain and darkness to deal with, and without his light—he had lost the damn thing somewhere—he had to slow his pace. Either that, or risk running headlong into a tree, and the footing in the wet leaves as treacherous as before.

He finally had to stop, grasping his knees as he drew huge and heaving breaths. *Can't be much further…if I've been going the right way.*

It was while catching his breath that he realized the burning pain from all the briar cuts he had suffered had receded to the point that it was almost nonexistent. He checked himself as best he could, again wishing he had the fucking light, and found only a few scrapes and scratches and all of them minor. So fighting his way through that thicket had never really happened? Had any of it—beyond the dead hooker and Robbie, the poor dumb bastard—really happened?

He found it easy to think he had imagined it all.

If only he could convince himself of that.

No time to be thinking like this. He could figure all this shit out once he was back home and a couple of cold beers in him. As soon as he could manage it, he was moving again.

It turned out that he was heading in the right direction. He discovered this when he came to the ditch he and Robbie had followed coming in. And it was the right one; he recognized it—finally, he recognized something! —and he almost fell in it before he could stop in time.

Goddamned the rain and wet leaves!

All his instincts were screaming at him to keep going, but he had to catch his breath again. He used the pause to listen for anything fucking weird that he shouldn't be hearing, but all he heard was the patter of rain. Again, he had to wonder if all that frightening shit had really happened. Or was he the victim of some self-induced mind fuck? Or maybe it was all like a freaky mirage, not really there to begin with?

Questions he couldn't stay focused on, as none of it seemed important. All that he cared about, all that mattered now, was leaving this place.

Keeping the ditch to his right and in sight the whole way, he reached the clearing and, with a feeling of relief he had never before experienced, found his car. Best of all, the car was as he had left it, the trunk lid still up. *Now if the motherfucker will just start.*

It took several tries, some inventive cussing and pounding the dashboard a couple of times, but the Caprice finally started with a loud and dirty fart from the tailpipe. *Got to replace the battery and starter before they quit on me altogether.* And, right now, thanks to the forced generosity of the dead hooker, he had the money to replace both.

Man, that first cold beer is going to be so fucking good.

He backed the car up, got it pointed right; switched on the one working headlight. Then he shifted into drive and was about to step on the gas when…

…*you've got to be shitting me.* A wave of cold swept through him that killed any hopeful thought he still entertained of mirages or imagination.

She stood in the centre of the dirt road, perhaps twenty yards in front of the car. A tiny and slight figure, slightly to one side of and just visible in the headlight's single beam. More of a shadow, an unnatural extension created by the light, than a shape of solid form. But there was no mistaking the dark hair, the long black dress, her head down and her face not clearly evident.

Above the rough idle of the Caprice's engine, Brad could hear, very faintly, the sound of fiendish laughter. His heart racing and pounding in his chest, he began shaking all over.

Only when her saw her head lifting, her face becoming clearer…

"Whatever you do, don't look her straight in the face!" Lanie's last words.

"If you do look her in the face and she screams?" Robbie had warned. *"Might as well kiss your ass good-bye because you'll soon be one of us."*

So it all did really happen…and she's real—

…was he able to tear his eyes away from her.

—but you haven't got me yet, bitch!

Only when he had jammed his foot on the accelerator, the Caprice's engine howling in protest—*just drive past her! Hell, just drive right over the bitch!*—did he risk a quick glance through the windshield. *What the fuck?*

The dark-haired figure was gone, the road empty. *Where did she go?*

Fuck it, goddamn it, just go! Just get the hell away from here!

He gave the accelerator another, harder push; the car bucked, the engine sputtering. Then there was a loud backfire and the engine stalled and died. There was a strong odour of gasoline.

The carburettor had flooded!

"*Shit!*"

He slammed on the brakes, the car sliding

a bit in the wet leaves, then stopped with a neck-snapping jerk. He shifted into park, then began frantically keying the ignition, the engine turning over weakly. *Start, you lousy bitch! Start!* The smell of gas was stronger; the engine wouldn't start, the battery rapidly losing what fire it had left. He kept at it until the engine refused to turn over at all, the spots of colour of the dash lights flickering and growing weaker.

Leaving him with only one option for escape. He was a second away from throwing open the door and fleeing on foot, when…

…there was a loud crack and a groaning creak of splintering wood, the sounds coming from his right. He saw movement through the right-side windows, a shadow falling toward the car. *A fucking tree!* Even as his mind registered this fact the tree hit the car with a rending of metal, the impact so violent that it threw him against the steering wheel. The black glass and both rear side windows exploded in a shower of fragments; he felt the sting of what seemed like dozens of cuts on his head and neck and back.

Fuck me! Dazed though he was, his mind quickly shook it off—*what the fuck made that tree come down like that?*—and was again trying to get the driver's side door open. But it was jammed shut; even throwing his shoulder against it several times as hard as he could didn't get the door open. Finally, shifting position as best he could and bringing up his feet, he kicked at the window until it shattered. *Yes, goddamn it!*

He was reaching for the opening, ready to pull himself out of the car, when a hand—*a fucking hand!*—gripped his shoulder. The fingers were like the jaws of a steel trap, the hands so cold that the chill spread through his shirt and he felt his shoulder and arm going numb.

But that chill was nothing compared to the one that almost stilled his heart when he heard the soft, fiendish laughter coming from the passenger seat. A second of frozen silence once the laughter had faded away, then…

"Such an evil man," a woman said, her voice an insidious whisper. "And a foolish one to think you could run me over and kill what's already dead." More of the fiendish laughter, then, "No, more games, Bradley Moore. Look at me."

"Fuck you," Brad mumbled in a low moan of fear. He refused to turn his head toward the voice, his eyes clamped shut. Even when the grip of fingers increased, like the hand was trying to rip away a large chunk of his shoulder, he refused to open his eyes or turn his head.

"Go ahead, tough guy," snapped a peevish, even impatient voice from outside the car. "Open your damned eyes and see the fate waiting for you."

Evie, he realized, the dead hooker. He opened his eyes; they were filled with terror as he stared through the windshield. The blonde and naked and bloody-faced bitch stood in front of the car; by the one headlight he could see the satisfied glare in her dead eyes. Beside her stood Robbie, his face an even ghastlier shade of blueish-grey, and yet it bore an unmistakable look of pity. On either side of and slightly behind them were his father and mother. Despite their badly burned faces, he knew it was his parents; he could tell it by the eyes. There was wisps of smoke rising from their charred corpses, but those eyes were filled with blank and indifferent glares he remembered all too well.

Then he heard the gentle sobbing of a child that was coming from his left. He looked toward the broken window and couldn't hold back the gasp that tumbled across his trembling lips as he stared at Lanie. Even in the near darkness in which she stood he knew it was her, and he could see the faintly glistening lines of moisture streaming down her cheeks.

"Look at me, Bradley," cooed the terrible voice beside him.

When he again refused to obey her command, her one hand still gripping his shoulder, he felt her other press to his face. He tried to resist her and her insistent hand but quickly realized that he was no match against the strength with which she forced his head around. It felt like she could easily snap his neck. He tried to close his eyes, but realized he couldn't even do that, as if she was exerting some sort of force that prevented it.

Completely helpless and at the mercy of whatever she had in mind...

He found himself staring straight into a dark and mysterious face. A face unravaged by death and still beautiful and framed by her glossy dark hair. Yet it was her eyes that stole what breath he had left. Hooded eyes that burned with such intense heat that he could feel the scorch of it on his skin. Even as she leaned closer, her lips parting as if she intended to kiss him, he could feel the heat of her stare building and building. He begin to squirm in her grip.

Then her mouth opened wide; the scream that ripped from her throat was piercing and impossibly loud, her breath like the heat from a blast furnace that hit him flush in the face. He only heard the scream for a split-second; that was long enough for it to rupture both eardrums. The sudden pain in his head was as searing as the tiny flames, stoked by the heat of her breath, that billowed to life near his neck and the top of his shirt.

He began thrashing in her grip, the pain in his head unbearable; the flames spreading down his chest and both arms. The flames fully engulfed him in only seconds. Black smoke, most of it unseen in the darkness, began belching in thick and cloying clouds from inside the smashed car.

The audience of the dead, only one of whom cried for the wicked man he had become, watched as he burned behind the wheel of his car. Deaf and in the throes of unspeakable pain, Brad was unable to hear the horrible screams of agony issuing from his own mouth.

Screams that seemed to fill the night.

Then the screams abruptly stopped, and there was only the crackle of flames, the sizzle of burning flesh, and the sound of fiendish laughter.

FOOTSTEPS

'What do you mean he's fucking dead?'

An argument somewhere far away, drifted from outside and into the waiting area, where the Lionel sat alone.

Lionel looked up at the television screen where a film he couldn't remember the name of, was playing. He wondered why there was no sound and then felt angry for even contemplating something so trivial. He let his hands support his head. All that existed now were the distant sounds of muffled voices and the white tiles on the floor.

Am I dreaming, is this a hospital…?

'Is there something I can do for you?' someone asked.

He looked up and saw a young black nurse staring down at him. Her smile seemed to flicker when she looked into Lionel's grey, heavy-set eyes. He wondered for a moment what she was thinking. If perhaps she could see the pain. Her awkwardness made him feel guilty. She was beautiful.

'I'll be close by if you need me,' she said and walked away.

He smiled and shook his head. Out of sight, the argument had ceased.

The room was empty. For an accident emergency, it should have been full, but there was no one. In the corner of the room a vending machine glowed. Nearby, stood a potted plant, that looked fake.

Lionel rubbed his tired face.

Something has happened?

What did I do?

Lionel turned around and saw the entrance doors were open. The night air would be perfect about now he thought.

Maybe it'll make me remember?

*

Outside the cold air felt good.

And there was no one, which he thought was a blessing as he made his way along the pathway leading to the gates. The only sounds were his shoes as they clicked loudly on the concrete. A man that has loud shoes is a confident man, his father had told him. He didn't feel very confident now.

He stopped at the gates and lit a cigarette,

which tasted surprisingly good.

There was no traffic. The streets were all sleeping. He thought about ordering a taxi and then decided it was better to walk. He glanced down instinctively to look at his watch but it was broken. The white face was cracked and he could see tiny gold cogs behind its panel. His father had left him that watch. Now he felt guilty.

How the hell did I break it?

Crossing the road, he moved up and further away from the hospital until it became a cluster of bleeding lights on the horizon.

He wasn't sure, but somehow he felt people were talking about him inside the place. He wondered if that nurse was talking to anyone about him.

*

The walk was doing him good.

He couldn't remember the last time he had walked this far. The hospital was long gone now and he had just passed the point of his familiar surroundings.

Suddenly a sickness filled him, pushing upwards from his balls right into his guts. The idea of why and how he could leave everyone behind scared him. No matter what had happened, he should have gone back home and explained it to Sandra. *But what has happened?*

'Look out!' someone shouted.

He looked around and then realised he was alone and the voice came from within.

He pushed the thought away and then Sandra made her way into his head.

The thought of Sandra made him retch. She was out there somewhere. She wouldn't be scared yet, wouldn't be worried that he hadn't returned home. She might have his tea in the oven, or be waiting for him to come home, so they could order takeout and stay up late; watch that shitty reality show she adores.

It was too late to turn back now.

*

He had been walking over an hour when he heard it. At first, he thought it was an echo of his own shoes, but by the time he turned into a street called Blakey Avenue, it had become obvious that someone was following him.

Why would you think that?

Someone was getting closer. Their sharp foot falls didn't sound far away.

I shouldn't have left the hospital. I shouldn't have gone. There were questions that needed answering and I fled.

He stopped suddenly.

From behind him there was nothing.

No footsteps.

He listened and just when he thought it was perfect silence, he heard the footsteps but only now they had turned to a light running.

He was too scared to turn around. Not too scared to run though, he thought and did just that.

This is the wrong thing to do.

Running will make it worse.

You've seen what happens on television to people that run.

They'll catch you for sure now. It's just a matter of time.

Or was it; it seemed the running behind him was getting slower. Whoever was chasing was getting tired.

He quickly speeded up his pace until. . .

'You have to stop sometime Lionel,' shouted a voice behind him.

'*Lionel!*'

Suddenly he felt his whole body shudder.

That voice - it was a woman's and it almost sounded familiar.

'Come on Lionel. You can't run forever,' said the voice, almost laughing.

Lionel glanced back quickly and saw a figure moving quickly towards him from the shadows. Its footsteps were uneven, like a drunk's. Like this was all some sort of game.

'Let's stop all this fooling around Lionel,' shouted the figure, sounding almost joyful.

Lionel stopped.

Listening as the footsteps got closer behind him.

Then there was a hand on his shoulder and Lionel froze.

The figure behind him didn't even sound out of breath. Still, Lionel took his chances and turned quickly on his heels, pushing the stranger to the floor, not daring to look into the darkness at who it might be.

Before he knew it, he was running, running as fast as he could, cursing himself at the same time.

Did I just push a woman?

He left Blakey Avenue and found himself in a city.

He made his way up another street, glancing behind him to see if the stranger was following but there was nothing.

He walked for awhile and then stood in a shop doorway concealed by shadows.

The only sound now was the tiny hum of the street lamps. There was nothing else in the whole world.

Sandra he thought. She'd be worried. Now it was only a matter of time before she would know about him.

And then what?

What would she think?

Slowly he slid down the shop door and hunkered, his hands clasped together.

Then he began to cry – and for a minute he wasn't sure he could stop. His mind raced. Before the hospital, he had been going somewhere. He remembered getting ready in his house, brushing his hair in the mirror and splashing on the cheap Denim aftershave that was ten years out of date.

But where was I going?

*

A little time had passed before he was wiping his

face and standing up ready to move again. He'd used the time well to think about Sandra. Damn, he missed her, which was crazy because he was sure it wasn't that long ago that he had seen her. Now of course, it was the time to start moving again before…

Suddenly there was a flash of yellow. Lionel quickly stepped out of the doorway and saw a dog, a big golden retriever.

It was stood in the middle of the road, its huge tongue hanging from its mouth to one side and its big black teardrop eyes watching him.

Studying.

God he thought, the last time he'd seen a dog like that had been when he was fourteen and it had been his pet Skip.

Slowly the beast walked across the road towards him.

Lionel didn't move as the dog got closer. Slowly he bent down on tired knees and stroked the dog's large head, feeling almost better when it reached up and licked its long pink tongue across his chin.

But something felt wrong.

The dog didn't only look like Skip, now he was sure it smelt like his old dog too.

He looked under the dog's head saw a blue collar with a silver badge hanging from it. The name **SKIP** carved crudely into it.

There was no way this dog could have been his. Skip had died of Leukaemia over twenty years ago.

Slowly he reached out for the badge and turned it over.

His old home number was on the back.

It was there, just like it had always been.

Lionel let go of the badge and began walking away.

He expected the dog to follow but there was nothing. He turned around and watched until it fell out of sight.

*

Walking was good; it was certainly clearing his head, or perhaps the dog had done that. Either way, it was better to think of a stupid dog than to think about Sandra because just imagining her made his heart ache.

I didn't see it, there were no lights or anything, said a voice in his head, one he didn't recognise.

He continued walking, not looking at any of the shop doorways but keeping his eyes forward, concentrating although not sure when would be the best time to stop his journey.

He knew he would have to stop at some point and then suddenly…

His shoes weren't making the loud claps as they hit the cement. Now the ground had become soft, like marsh.

He looked down and saw to his amazement that the road had turned to wet leaves and mud. In front of him huge trees soared way up above, opening into a forest.

How hadn't I seen this before?

He turned around and looked back up the street. It didn't make any sense. Why would a street suddenly end abruptly for a forest? A street light glowed amber from the edge of the forest and Lionel quickly dismissed any stupid childish ideas of Narnia.

He looked around.

There seemed no where else to go, everything seemed to lead to this one point.

He entered the forest and that was when he heard the laughing. He recognised it instantly and it made him shiver in fear. His sister came to mind.

Suddenly from the forest he heard her again.

Nancy.

He hadn't thought about Nancy since he was...

He couldn't remember. It was like he had actually forgotten. He remembered the last time he'd seen her. It had been in a forest just like this one. He had been seven or eight and she had been six. She used to always have a mouthful of red rope. She loved sweets but those were her favourites.

And that's why she died.

It was his mother's voice in his head now. He didn't want to hear it but there it was.

He looked up and was shocked to see the dark sky had changed to grey with morning – which seemed impossible since he couldn't have left the hospital later than eleven.

*

'Give me some sweets' that's what he'd shouted at her as they made their way together into the woods that day.

Keep an eye on her – his mother had told him, and he nodded without thinking.

She'd wanted to see the swing he'd been building. It was in the middle of Walters Woods, near to where they'd lived.

He had built a swing with Gavin Gatelock a few days before Gavin got the stomach bug and couldn't leave the house. That's why he'd come here with his sister, because all his other friends either had the bug or were away for the summer. If Gavin had been okay, perhaps Nancy wouldn't be dead.

They'd been fighting because he wouldn't let her ride THE WORLD WIND; god that's what the kids had called it. The swing was nothing more than a line of thick blue rope tied to a thick branch from an old Oak tree hanging down to a stump of a branch where they'd sit. Lionel and Gavin had spent hours putting the rope in between their legs and sitting on the branch. They could get a great height on the thing too, clearly seeing right across Ouston, and on a clear day, all the way to Pelton Fell. Back then, when summer holidays with friends would last forever.

But on this day, there was only him, and Nancy who wouldn't stop crying to have a go and wouldn't give up her last red rope.

She cried crocodile tears shouting and calling him a fart stain, a word she copied from Gavin.

In the end Lionel had let her have a go on the swing, if only to shut her up.

She smiled when he offered her the branch and took it from him. She lifted her red dress and stuck the wood in between her legs. In her mouth, a long length of red rope hung like a snake's tongue.

As she began to walk backward into position she took the sweet from her mouth and offered it to Lionel and that was the last happy image he had of his sister - her smiling face staring at him. Her kindness that day would upset him for the rest of his life.

So, he'd taken the red rope and put it in his pocket to give it back because the idea of taking her last sweet had made him feel guilty, even more guilty now she had given him it for a go of his stupid swing.

She flew passed him and over the ravine which dropped about ten feet into bramble bushes, that could soften the blow if you fell, but also hurt like hell.

Lionel watched her fly through the air screaming and laughing, her red hair flowing behind her like spun gold. He often wondered in hindsight if the rope wouldn't have snapped had he not glanced up at the tree branch and saw it was fraying.

He'd tried to warn her when he saw it happening, but before the words had left his mouth…

His kid sister was flying through the air, unaware that she wasn't going to be swinging back.

By the time she realised her body was twisted half turning to look back. Lionel ran forward to the edge of the ravine and watched her descent in slow motion. Just before impact, her body twisted again and Lionel froze stiff on seeing she was falling headfirst.

Nancy screamed all the way down until impact. Too scared to look over the ravine, Lionel ran as fast as he could back to his house and told his parents. By the time they returned, Nancy Underwood was dead. But it wasn't a broken neck that had killed her. In fact, she hadn't broken any bones. It was a small piece of her favourite sweet she'd been chewing when she landed, that had lodged in her throat. Lionel took the piece from his pocket she had given him, her bite marks still glistening on the end where she'd snapped a mouthful off.

Lionel often lay in bed wondering, if he hadn't run away he might have some how been able to save her. He wasn't the only one that thought that. His mother's eyes told him the same thing, every time Nancy was brought up in conversation.

*

He wasn't even sure this was the same forest. Of course it wasn't, how could it be?

He walked forward a few more paces and then he saw it. The rope swing gently swaying from the tree. And there she was in her red dress, not yet moving.

Quickly he began to run towards her and half expected her to leap out over the ravine and he'd be forced to watch her die again.

But she didn't.

She just sat there and when he got close enough he knew why.

She already was dead. He walked closer and saw her face, a dark shade of purple, with closed bulging eyes.

He wanted to tell her he was sorry but as he got within arm's-length her eyes opened and stared at him. They were bloodshot and she couldn't have possibly seen him, but she did. She was looking straight at him.

'Give me back my red rope, Lionel,' she said, sounding cross.

Lionel felt his head swimming. Everything felt like it was swimming. He stumbled forward, towards her and pushed himself backwards.

Through blurred vision, she was lifting

herself from the swing and walking towards him and with each step, there was a choking sound as she gasped for breath.

'Give me my red rope, Lionel,' she said, her voice sounding watery and thin.

Lionel turned and started trying to move away from his sister.

'You can't run forever my friend!' said another voice behind him.

Lionel's head suddenly cleared and when he looked back there she was, the woman who had been chasing him all along. She was dressed in a long black dress, not like she had been at the hospital. Maybe she wasn't a nurse, thought Lionel.

He quickly looked back at his sister but she was gone. The rope swing gently swaying in the breeze.

'Get away from me!' shouted Lionel at the woman.

'You need to come with me Lionel, this isn't good for you.'

'I'm sorry I pushed you, I know you're a cop or something, but I don't know what the hell it is I've done.'

And with that he started running again. He

didn't look back to see if the woman was following, although he was sure she was.

He made his way through the forest and onto a street. A street he instantly recognised. It was where he'd lived, his first flat with Sandra before they'd got the house. Without hesitation, he wiped the sweat from his face and started walking towards the old place.

He didn't expect to find the bottom floor flat door open but it was. He walked inside and was hit by the smell of the place. The smell he sometimes remembers just before he goes to sleep.

Up stairs he could hear laughing. He could hear her laugh.

He walked up the stairs in twos and opened the living room door.

The room was filled with people, all his friends. Across the walls balloons and banners were hung.

Happy 21st Lionel.

He smiled, as a sudden warmth he hadn't felt for a long time, washed over him. Chris Barber was talking to a group of people, showing off about his job and that somehow made Lionel want to cry. Ramones played on the cd player. Jamie McDermott was standing chatting with her friends looking as good as he remembered her from college. And then there was Sandra, the only woman he'd ever loved. Slowly, he walked through the crowd towards her.

But she couldn't see him.

How could she?

Lionel walked closer and he felt if he dared to touch her, that he might push a hand straight through her like in that awful movie.

Slowly he walked away, unsure of what was happening.

Joey Ramone was singing about a girl called Sheena but the sound was fading and not just from the music. The laughter was fading, and then all his friends faded until the room was empty and there was only Lionel and the woman from the hospital. She stood against the bookcase smiling tenderly at him.

'What is happening to me?'

The woman walked towards him.

If she touches me, I can't let her touch me, thought Lionel.

The woman had a lingering aroma to her. Lionel had never smelt a corpse rotting before, but he was sure that was what the woman smelt of.

And then he was running again, out of the room and down the stairs, his chest thumping with panic and fear. He flung the door open and raced into the street and stopped suddenly…

The street wasn't there.

He was somewhere else.

There were bright flashing blue lights everywhere. There were cars everywhere and there were people.

Lionel walked into the crowd and saw a bus stop had been smashed to the ground. Close by was a white Ford Ka lying on its side, completely written off.

Lionel walked closer. At the bus stop, there was a woman crying. No, she was screaming, 'What do you mean he's fucking dead?'

Lionel got closer. He didn't recognise her, which felt good. Two policemen were holding her back and he heard one shout, 'Where is the ambulance?'

He walked closer and knew before reaching the body that it was his.

Lionel felt his stomach turn. He could see a long line of blood pouring from behind his own waist down the street in a long glistening line. Shards of his watch lay on the cement like tiny diamonds.

Suddenly everything was obvious.

He turned around looking for the woman

in black.

'It would have been easier if you hadn't left the hospital. You know that now,' she said as she stepped up beside him.

'I'm sorry' whispered Lionel 'I guess I walked there thinking I could be saved.'

'That's okay. Most do the same.'

'Where am I?'

'Lost in a world that is no longer yours I'm afraid,' she said, sounding sympathetic.

'This is my life?'

'No this is your death. It's how you died. Waiting for a bus, when the woman over there lost control of her car and hit you.'

'I'm sorry I pushed you?'

'Oh forget about it. One little push doesn't mean much. I've been shot, stabbed and set on fire twice.'

'Was there any chance I might have escaped you?'

'Of course there was. Then you'd have been drifting through your life for eternity. You might have visited some good times, but you would have felt a deep sadness all the while. The place I take you is your home now. I promise,

Lionel, you'll find peace.'

'Am I going up or down?'

The woman in black laughed and placed a hand on Lionel's shoulder.

'You've seen too many movies,' she said. 'You'll see, but how's about we grab a quick drink first.'

'Can we do that?'

'Course we can, don't you know who I am?' she said smiling and suddenly he knew. He knew exactly who the woman was and as they walked, he asked her questions about his life, and when the woman answered him, he no longer felt afraid and when he asked if he could say goodbye to Sandra, she said 'Sure, why not.'

THE EMPORIUM IS YOURS

The boy didn't know how long had gone by. It felt like hours, or perhaps days, no wait. The sky had gone from dark to blue a dozen times hadn't it? Food had come and gone like the cars outside. Artaud had cast spells that vanquished the old and fresh food would appear.

Arn looked down. His hands were no longer young and the skin wasn't tight. They looked crumpled and old.

Old.

The boy felt his face, it was thick with hair.

How long have I been here he wondered? Across the table lay the dead stranger, his mouth hung open mid sentence. Inside it nothing but darkness. The wonderful porcelain skin had been replaced. It had faded and reminded Arn of cracked paint.

'What have you done to me?' asked the boy. 'How long have I been sat here listening to your stories?'

Yet Arn the man knew. He knew everything. He knew all about Earth and its tales of wonderment – the stranger had even taken relics of his favourite ones. He knew in other universes the earth was in danger from terrible creatures, and in another the Earth was dying because of strange lights in the sky. He liked the world he was in now best, the one he had learned about the boy who hung out at cemeteries and people who waited for phone calls from the long-departed dead. This world had hope.

Slowly with cracking limbs Arn stood up. He looked down at his long-time companion. Artaud was pointing a long bone china finger across the room. The boy followed it to a glass case. Stuck on top was a piece of parchment. The boy walked towards it and picked it up. In the case beneath, a slug-like creature stopped pulsating and rose to look up through the glass. The elegant red plinth it rolled on was covered in slug sweat. Arn covered it with the parchment and read.

'These are your stories now Arn. You know them all. The best and worst of this world. Your role is to keep them and gather more and when you can't gather more, you must recruit someone that can. It doesn't have to be a man like you or a Nigh like me, it can be anyone worthy of listening. Like I found you worthy because you have a wonderful gift. You never forget a story. You never forgot your mother. Go on and find more stories to record. One day we will need them. Bring them back to your Emporium. But remember not all tales are woven from this place. You might want to venture further and discover other worlds. My magic is now

yours. You've absorbed it over time.'

Arn dropped the parchment and walked to the window. The food had tasted good, too good. He looked down at his finger tips and saw they shone bright with magic.

The stranger had showed him such sights in this world, told him so many great tales. Perhaps he would find more here, or maybe he would travel. Find a new world with just as exciting, macabre and fascinating tales.

After all a good story, can be found anywhere

It's just waiting to be heard.

COPYRIGHT RICHARD ALAN LONG 2019

Printed in Poland
by Amazon Fulfillment
Poland Sp. z o.o., Wrocław